The Siren's Secret

The Siren's Secret

Justine Brown

TIN PRESS • LONDON

Also by this author

Non-fiction

All Possible Worlds:
Utopian Experiences in British Columbia
(New Star Books)

Hollywood Utopia
 (New Star Books)

Also from Tin Press

Where the English Housewife Shines
Alexandra Oliver (poetry/humor)

The Longest Day of the Year
Phil Smith/Corsage (poetry/lyrics/photography)

Praise for Justine Brown's *Hollywood Utopia*

"Brown creates a vivid picture of a...world apart ... a fascinating oddity"
- The Globe and Mail

"an entirely surprising book...A story that shimmers with bright unreality, like a mirage fueled by a heated road"
- The Stranger

"Deftly written...never less than interesting and refreshing"
**- Robert Sklar, New York Univerity
in Labour/La Travail**

Please send any enquires to info@tin-press.com

Tin Press
www.tin-press.com

11 Rudolf Place
Miles Street
London, England
SW8 1RP

11835 SE Yamhill Street
Portland, Oregon
97216
USA

Artwork by Dame Darcy
(www.damedarcy.com)
Typeset by Tin Press
Editing credits and many thanks go to Joan Haggerty, Jessica Glenn and Hugh Brown and of course Dame Darcy for her beautiful work

ISBN: 978-0-9835270-1-5

CATALOGUING IN PUBLICATION DATA
Brown, Justine 1965-
The Siren's Secret

1. Back to the Land Movement - British Columbia - History. 2. First Nations Mythology.
3. Sir Francis Drake - Travels in the Pacific Northwest. 4. Countercultures.

Dame Darcy

Still she haunts me, phantomwise/Alice moving under skies...
Lewis Carroll,
Through the Looking-Glass

Chapter One

Sappho Smith was curled up tight in the back of the juddering VW van, treading the frontiers of sleep, when she first heard her mother mention the fairy.

"When does the fairy come?" her mom, who was at the wheel, asked Billy Black. And later, "we have to catch that fairy." Which sounded strange, and Sappho wondered blearily why a fairy, such a delicate airborne being, should have to be trapped. The van climbed higher and the fog gathered them in, as though they were driving up to the clouds, like an airplane. Soon the remarks grew more urgent, and as the white darkness came down they drove more rapidly, the streetlights flooding the van with sulphur-yellowish light at faster and faster intervals, whoosh-whoosh, whoosh-whoosh.

"I sure do hope that fairy is late," Sappho's mother said anxiously. "'Cause we sure are."

"I bet we get 'er," said Billy. "She'll be there all right." Sappho closed her eyes and saw the slender silvered fairy, flying with all the might of her luminous veined wings to meet them, flying high and hard. Sappho squeezed her lids and beamed a message out into the nightscape: we're coming. Hold.Tight. Hold... "Sleep now," came a voice from somewhere. "Sleep tight." And the dreams descended again.

They were driving north, to Gray Star. Sappho and her mom had left New York—the Big Smoke, as Billy called the city, any city— and returned to her mother's home town. Now they were moving again and leaving even green Vancouver behind. They were abandoning city life altogether and going Back to the Land, a perfect place where Mom could make a garden with flowers and vegetables, and have another baby—and everything— and Sappho could run wild and free in the forest. That's what Mom said. No electricity, no furnaces, no store-bought food, no tv...which meant no Saturday morning cartoons and no *Batman*, but they might have some pigs and sheep. They hadn't known Billy very long, only four months, but Mom said they were going to live at his place in the country. They hadn't known him long, but he made Sappho's heart burst with his smiling. Mirroring his cheer, she would wordlessly beg him to stay with them, stay. He would point at her, blond eyebrows like furred caterpillars, growling "I warn ya, baby, it'll be rough in The Bush!". When his smile cracked wide, Sappho's face opened too.

"We'll be pioneers. It'll be like *Little House on the Prairie*," Sappho's mother whispered at bedtime, her whisper full of promise. "But not so cold. They say it hardly ever snows." That sounded pretty good. She would wear a bonnet and a muslin dress and lace-up boots.

Billy Black told Sappho he was a student, though with his big beard he looked way too much like a dad for that. An *archaeology* student, he explained, and taught Sappho to spell it. He was a graduate student. "Diggin' up old Indians," he said. "Diggin' up their ways." Billy Black was from California. Sappho wondered why he would leave Disneyland to come here. He told them he had come North in '69.

"Are you a landed immigrant now?" asked Kathleen meaningly.

"*Stranded* immigrant, more like!" replied Billy in his gravelly way. And Kathleen, a little offended on behalf of Canada, said in a soft, dignified voice that he could probably get amnesty if he wanted to get back to the States so much. That was on offer now, apparently. But Billy laughed and rasped merrily that he'd better not dare show his sorry ass back at Berkeley without Sir Francis Drake in tow, whatever that meant. Nah, said Billy, the life of a student was sweet. And he'd gotten used to living here. In Gray Star, British Columbia, Canada. In Gray Star.

Billy had little round gold-framed eyeglasses and a big foamy blond beard; parts of his face emerged above the dense yellow underbrush— his nose, for example. He wore a soft thick plaid work-shirt in red and black, its pockets packed with pens, notebooks and littler note-books. He wore a fringed suede vest, thick brown cord trousers and gumboots with thick gray fisherman's socks, the kind with a ring of neon orange at the top; he carried a gold pocket watch on a long chain. Billy's clothes were dense, saturated, with woodsmoke and sawdust and pipe tobacco. He smelled strong, sort of *cured*. When Billy wasn't on the dig out at the local Indian reserve, thinking about the Indians, writing about the Indians or following the local ones around, he did odd carpentry jobs. Billy had built the house they would all share. In the forest, near Gray Star. Sappho prayed that they would live with Billy forever.

The sun woke Sappho, poking pink-gold fingers into her greenish eyes. She sat up, yawning and rubbing the sleep-sand away with her fists. Noticing she was awake, Billy unfolded a large map, shook it out, and traced his pipe-stem along the lace of filigreed lines and fragments of land among the pale blue. "See, the fairy, she'll take us right through here, past Bone Island and towards Seashell, the Sunshine Coast..."

With a groan and a shudder the VW van rounded the corner and bore down into Horseshoe Bay. Struggling with the gear-shift, Mom gave an urgent little shout: "The fairy! The fairy's here!"

And Billy yelled "*theeere* she is! Far-fuckin'-out!"

Anxiously, Kathleen whispered "*Cool it with the language, babe. She's young.*"

Sappho peered out excitedly into the brightening dawn, but she couldn't see the fairy. What she *did* see was a gigantic white-and-blue ship tucked snug in a harbour. A long line of cars was disappearing into it. Behind the ship was the dark satiny gray-blue inlet, with islands thick-quilled with deep dark greenery, and mountains stretching deep blue and cooler, cooler, beyond that. Atop the on-ramp a little figure in a neon-orange quilted vest and gumboots beckoned them on. Down, down the hill they plunged, into the wide mouth of the ship.

Gulls meowed plaintively all around the harbour.

Gray Star, British Columbia, is a typical coastal town, no more ravishing in summer, no darker when the long rains come, than any other such coastal BC town. The town is bisected by a wide, deep river, a salmon run;

at its mouth, where sweet water mingles with the salt, stretches a two-lane bridge. It's got a pulp mill nearby, Gray Star Pulp & Paper, which employs most of the locals most of the time. A pulp mill, an ice rink, a dim little mall. And an Indian reserve. The reserve, that other place, stretches along the water behind the SuperStar Mall. There's a longhouse there, some churches, and a lot of tiny box-shaped houses— one candy-pink, one pale yellow, another sky-blue— that sit a bit lop-sidedly in the raw dirt. No-one bothers much with lawns on the reserve. Big shabby luxury cars are parked at odd angles to the houses. Toys and kids' bikes are scattered around like rubble. No-one bothers much with the accumulated garbage. At the shoreline is a midden, with layer upon layer of broken shells and other things, who knows exactly how deep. The tribe has been there for who knows exactly how long— thousands of years before the town was named Gray Star, anyway.

The fog comes and goes, and forms materialize suddenly like icebergs out of nowhere. Across the slatey water you can often see the mountains of Vancouver Island stretching gray-blue in the distance. And at night, when it's overcast, the lights of a town on the Island stand in for the stars. When it's cloudy, which is most of the time. But when it's not, the stars hover near; they burn clear and white and bright and close. And in the star-storms of August they rain down like a child's sparkler, without burning the flesh.

In summer the coast highway is a long parade of idling camper vans, trailers and RVs pouring off the ferry, and the summer people triple the population. Gray Star, like the whole B.C. coast, is irresistible in the hot season, and half the tourists vow to come back there for good. They picture returning to Red Deer, Alberta or Barrie, Ontario just long enough to shutter their brick houses and settle their affairs, dreaming an endless parade of soft gold days on the coast. The air is blackberry-sweet and sea-salty there, and the deep undergrowth of the woods a cool miraculous green. There is yellow-blooming broom and flesh-tinted, smooth-skinned arbutus at the water's edge. Purple starfish cling to the rocks. When sundown lends a mauve glow to the landscape the tide creeps up warm, over the rocks and silver-bleached logs that line the shore. The ocean creeps high, almost into the grass, and the people amble down to meet it. They come languid with summer pleasures, towels slung over their shoulders. They swim, and the seawater feels warmer than the cooling evening air.

It was like that the day they arrived. Chugging off the boat, Billy at the wheel now, the VW snaked along the Coast Highway behind a long line of camper vans. They drove past the Reserve. Kate asked a lot of questions about the tribe—were they very poor? Did any of them speak in the old tongue? Billy seemed content to play tour guide.

"What about their spiritual beliefs?"

"Aww, there're Catholics, Evangelicals, and some Angelicans—"

"You mean Anglicans, Billy?" Kate interrupted.

"Nope. An*geli*cans. As in angels. They believe that after God made the world, he got pissed off at mankind and abandoned ship. Left four archangels at the helm and got on with other projects."

"Wow."

"Yeah. For them, the creation is just kind of... adrift. And *all* the dead are in Limbo, hoping God will come back and sort 'em out."

"Amazing. How did—"

"Angelicanism spread among the Natives? Missionaries. Or rather, Messengers: that's what they called themselves. Came in the 1890s, I think. Their temple is on the Rez. It's called St. Zadkiel and Other Archangels."

"What about native traditions?"

"Well, they have their ways. There're carvers, and plenty of singers and dancers. Plus there's a bunch of tribe members—like my friend Dan Joe—who are trying to reconstruct the whole story cycle... pass it on to the kids. The elders know tons, but on the other hand, a lotta those tales have been lost.... I've been able to help out a bit in that department."

"You have?"

"I put Dan onto a nineteenth-century anthropologist. Scandinavian guy. He was one of the first white men to learn Sechelt and other Salish languages. Wrote down a whole lotta tales the elders recited."

Rounding a bay, they passed a small firehall ("Volunteer department," offered Billy. "A lot of us do it."). Then they drove by a neatly tended lawn upon which stood several people in white shorts, peering seaward through binoculars. "That's Lookout Park," Billy said. "People try to get a glimpse of the Siren, our local sea-beastie. The kind the Tourist Board likes. She gets spotted at the mouth of the river sometimes. Supposed to have a kind of sea-serpent's body and the face of a woman. And long inky hair."

"Sounds like a mermaid," said Sappho.

"'Siren' is another name for mermaid, actually," observed Kate.

"Yeah, well, the Indians have a different name for her, of course," said Billy. "It's hard to pronounce. There's a story behind her, I think. Got something to do with the Salmon Clan."

A bumpy bridge took them over the river.

Gradually the traffic thinned out. One by one, the camper vans and cars turned left or right and were swallowed up by the thick evergreen and alder forest that crowded close to the highway on both sides. On their left, an occasional flash and sparkle told Sappho the ocean was there behind the trees, curving alongside the road. Kate made appreciative hums at regular intervals. As they passed a big hand-painted sign reading "Camp Gray Star" in big letters, Billy slowed the VW. "Kids say that place is pretty fun," he remarked. She saw a brightly painted totem pole among the trees, an eagle fanning his painted wings at the crown of it.

They turned off the highway. They drove about a mile up a narrow gravel road. Leathery salal leaves and salmon-berry bushes brushed against the sides of the VW, and cedar trees dangled their long arms into the windshield, dragging their fingers and sometimes elbowing too with alarming jabs.

"Welcome to Chickenland!" announced Billy, spinning the steering wheel hard right.

He drove the van into a clearing and braked with a lurch alongside an old pickup truck, sending stray red hens squawking in all directions. In the middle of the clearing stood a big white bathtub. Its brass lion paws were planted in embers: a wood fire was burning beneath it. In the bathtub, bathing in water and sunlight, sat a figure.

"Is that a lady?" asked Sappho.

"Good question," replied Billy, almost to himself. "Good. F— frigging. Question." The bather gazed at them. She had very long strawberry-blond hair, and her pale eyes were fringed thick with pale eyelashes, wet like anenomes. Her white flesh was dusted with freckles. She pinched her nose and arched backwards, disappearing from view. They got out of the VW and began dragging their luggage out too. The woman was still invisible. Sappho approached the tub and peered nervously over the rim. The mysterious bather floated below the surface of the water, her light red hair fanned out around her. Suddenly she surfaced, exhaling dramatically like a whale through its blowhole. She stood up and climbed out, streaming water everywhere. The embers sputtered and hissed and steamed.

"I am Galadriel," she said, her tones whispery and girlish. "Welcome to these woods."

Billy gave a snort. "Oh, shove *off*, *Nancy*. Take your lily-white ass back to *your* place."

The bather fixed the three of them with a riddling stare, water coursing over her white breasts, her stomach, her red tangle, her before she walked wetly away and vanished into the forest.

There was a small silence.

"Well, that's the cabin over there," Billy told them, his face frozen grim for a moment. He was pointing across the clearing at a house which was all peaked roof and no wall. Then he burst back into smiles and scooped up Sappho, sleeping bag and all. "Let's put your stuff up in the loft, kid."

Sappho now found herself in deep in the country for the first time. They had always lived in cities, cities that buzzed and hummed with electric life. But the country air tingled with noise too— the dense tangle of the insect metropolis. The forest was all athrob with insect wings; the honeyed air shook with insect stirrings and comings and goings, and the songbirds added their whoops and trills. And over all of this came a cackling chorus.

"Chickens," murmured Billy. His voice was tender.

Billy explained that the chickens were just settling into a newly built coop. Neatly shingled like the cabin and the sheds, the coop was nearly as big as the A-frame, and had windows with curtains and flower-boxes. There was also a front porch with benches, and the window-frames were gaily painted in purple and blue.

"Wow," marveled Sappho. "It sure is fancy."

"Yeah. Constant renovations— I figure it's the only way to keep 'em satisfied. They're always trying to move in with me." As they approached the coop the clucking grew louder, taking on a wary note. Low and dangerous don't-mess-with-me cluckings would suddenly explode into hysteria. Sappho, hugging herself for protection, wondered just how many chickens were in there. A red hen skittered out the door like a drunk chucked out of a bar. She gave herself a quick shake and regained composure, stepping off into the yard with a warning cluck.

It was followed by another red hen, then another and another. They stared sideways at the strangers, hazarding the odd peck at the ground, still clucking resentfully.

"Don't you keep them penned up, Billy?" asked Kathleen.

"Aw, no... I couldn't do that."

"But doesn't that make it hard to collect the eggs?"

Billy snorted. "That's fer *damn* sure. I never know *where* the heck they'll turn up! And the worst part is, the eggs're usually rotten by the time I find 'em." He shook his head in mock sorrow.

"But come on inside."

They stepped into their new home. A rust-red hen tried to barge in with them, and Billy gently but firmly shooed her out. Inside they smelled fresh-cut wood and woodsmoke, all things woody, and kerosene in the lamps dotted around the room. "Oh, Billy," marveled Kate, "This is *wonderful*. I feel I've escaped the twentieth century at last!"

There was a rope ladder leading to the loft. "Give it a shot, kid," urged Billy. "Just grab it and yard yourself up." Sappho hoisted herself and found the loft to be dominated by a gigantic mattress which lay on the floor with a kerosene lamp, rolling papers, a typewriter, and a stack of books beside it— books like *How to Build Your Home in the Woods* and *Wildflowers of British Columbia* and lots of others called things like *Prominent Myths of North-west Indians* and *Pirate or Privateer? Sir Francis Drake in the New World*. And a Tintin book! It was *Red Rackham's Treasure*, the cover showing Tintin and his dog Snowy exploring under pale green water. Sappho loved Tintin. She noted a few mildewed comic books lying there too, warped with the damp. The drawings didn't have the crispness of D.C. or Marvel. Those she would pick over more closely later.

"You'll sleep up here, darling," said Mom, coming up behind her.

Billy called up cheerfully: "We'll be downstairs. It's handier to the coop anyway. The chickens'll like it." But with their warbling warning clucks, they didn't sound easy to please.

Sappho climbed over the mattress to look out the window. Behind the A-frame she could see a puny bridge, no more than a plank really, leading to a tiny oblong building. Sappho was enchanted. "Could I live out there? In the other cabin?"

"If you can stomach the reek!" Billy giggled hoarsely from below.

"What cabin, sugar?" Kate asked in distracted tones, thumbing through the bookshelf.

"The one out back! With the little moon carved on the door!"

"It's the goddamn crapper!" sputtered Billy, doubled over with laughter. Tears of delight brimmed in his blue eyes.

"Oh dear," said Kathleen, giving Sappho a hasty refuge in her long wraparound cotton skirt.

Chapter Two

The crowing of the rooster scattered sleep, waking Sappho. She had grown used to this. Sunbeams were just starting to penetrate the deep evergreens. She could hear someone rapidly chopping wood, and crawled to the picture window for a look. Billy, his back to her, was raising his axe over a big chunk of orangey cedar. As he worked away, the pile of kindling mounted. It began to look like french fries to Sappho, whose rare trips to McDonald's— Kate had forbidden McDonald's, but Grandma had sometimes sneaked her there— had made a deep impression. Sappho was hungry now, and she was about to make for the rope ladder when she noticed a little boy at the edge of the clearing.

He looked about five. The pointy tips of his ears peeped out from his thatched white-blond hair. He was skinny, with narrow brown shoulders and arms emerging from a pair of overalls. His feet were bare too. The boy hovered at the edge of the clearing, and it seemed like the forest might draw him back in again at any moment. But then Billy stopped his swinging and, resting one leg on the chopping-block, raised a hand in greeting. The little boy waved back, and then, all hesitation gone, ran smiling towards the man. Billy gave him a quick strong hug; Sappho felt a small twinge. Who was this boy?

She crawled back into bed and buried herself in her book. It was *The Hobbit*, which Kate had given her just before they left Vancouver. Bilbo Baggins, scrambling around underground, had just found a ring, which he slipped on his finger. Sappho forgot about the boy and Billy, about her mother, the clearing and the forest around them. All Gray Star evaporated as Bilbo met Gollum for the first time.

There was a crash as the door opened. "Wake up, gals!" yelled Billy, "The boys've got wood, and if we've got wood, we've got fire! And if we've got fire, we've got... PANCAKES!" Peeking down from the loft, Sappho saw Billy and the boy, their arms full of the freshly chopped cedar. Billy ushered out two chickens that had sneaked in after them.

Kate gave her morning moan, a ritual noise that married sleepiness to real joy at the prospect of a new day. "Pancakes," she said, and then added, teasingly, "Is that the women's work?"

And then, "Oh, hello! And who might you be?"

"Well now, this fine gentleman is our neighbour. Nancy's kid." Sappho figured she'd better come down.

"What's your name, sweetie?" asked Kate.

The boy looked at her imploringly.

Billy said, "His mother— that crazy wi— bi— Nancy calls him *Glorfindel*. After some friggin' *elf*." Billy smiled at the boy; the boy smiled back. "But over here his name is Finn."

"Finn, is it?" The thin blond child nodded and hazarded a smile. "Finn it is then! Sappho, come down and meet our neighbour."

Everyone pitched in one way or another, and soon they were all four seated around the table and a tall stack of pancakes. The pancakes were whole wheat, nothing like Grandma's, but with all the butter and maple syrup that didn't seem to matter. The pancakes were delicious, and they kept coming. Billy was experimenting with shapes. He made Mickey Mouse pancakes, with two small dollops for ears. Finn ate faster than anyone, and kept holding out his plate for more helpings.

"Anyone'd think this kid hadn't eaten in weeks," said Billy. "Where's the Elf Queen Herself this morning? Where's Nancy?"

Finn stopped eating. "The door's closed. My mom says not to come in."

Kate asked in her careful way, "Not to come in where? Her room?"

"Yah."

Billy rolled his eyes and sighed. "Another lucky night at the Goon Saloon, I guess. Wonder who she magicked back this time. Poor donkey."

"*Billy*! Let's talk about this *later*." Kate was looking at Finn, whose silvery-blond head was bent over his plate. He was eating away again, seemingly oblivious.

Sappho hadn't been inside the Goon Saloon, but she had heard a lot about it. It was across the road from the Gray Star General Store, she knew. (That was where the hippies usually got their groceries. The "straights" always drove down the highway to shop at the SuperStar.) The Goon Saloon was over top of Bob's place— Blow-Yer-Brains-Out Bob, who had once tried to shoot his head off, but failed to die. His face was skewed now, but he smiled a lot. He had forgotten ever wanting to leave this world. Bob divided his waking hours between the General Store and the Goon Saloon, had a stool in each. A panting old black retriever accompanied him back and forth across the road.

The Goon Saloon opened when it opened and closed when it closed. The house band was a one-man affair: Cowboy Cal, a skinny guy in tight jeans who made his bed on a lumpy couch in the Goon Saloon. Cal was never seen without his black ten-gallon hat—to hide his balding scalp, Billy said. Cowboy Cal wore a big waxed mustache and could— with enough hard cider and smoke and a steady trickle of money to top up the coffee-can he kept under his stool—strum, pick and wail through dawn and well towards lunch. The hippies danced with enthusiasm, pleating their knees and elbows in time and sending up little howls and hoots of appreciation. The Goon Saloon balanced merriment with menace; sometimes the mood blackened sharply. Now and then, when a fight would break out, sending bottles and furniture— as well as the odd patron— flying against walls and out the windows and into the road, the local pair of Mounties showed up and ordered everyone off the premises. It was an unlicensed establishment, much of the booze was prepared in the saloon basement, and the air was soupy with home-grown weed. Sergeants Macleod and Stivitch would see everyone out, then nail the door shut and affix a notice to the door. After a day or two, the Goon Saloon would reopen. Eventually, a fight would break out.

After breakfast, after washing up, after Billy and Finn had chopped more wood and fed the chickens and done a little reno work on their coop— after all that, there was still no sign of Nancy. Billy and Finn drove down to the General Store for provisions. They had lunch. Then Billy slipped the children a tube of Lovehearts each, a finger at his lips and a sly glance over at Kate, who was washing the thick earth-brown pottery. Sappho ate six tangy discs, savouring the messages (CHASE ME 4 EVER MY BOY SWEET STUFF ALWAYS FOR KEEPS). She stashed the rest of the treasure in the loft under the mattress. Now no-one would steal it, and no-one would confiscate it either.

Finn, who couldn't read yet, gobbled all his candy at once. He chewed loudly, attracting Kate's attention.

"Say AH," she ordered, bending down towards him. Finn obeyed, displaying a tongue coated in partly chewed Lovehearts.

"Where did that come from?" Kate glanced in Billy's direction. Billy shrugged, his eyes bugging with innocence. Finn began giggling.

Kate leaned over and looked inquisitorially into Finn's merry eyes. "Where did you get that junk? Sugar's nothing but poison, you know. White death." Finn's giggling fit became a giggling jag, and soon he was rolling ecstatically on the floor. Sappho had never seen him so animated.

"Only five 'n already on drugs," said Billy, knitting his fuzzy yellow eyebrows in consternation.

"Thanks to *you*, I bet. Tsk." Kate shook her head and turned back to the dishes. Finn was still laughing. His cheeks were wet.

Some hours passed. "Come on, everyone, let's walk Finn home," called Billy, taking up the walking stick he had just finished carving. So off they trooped, out of the clearing and into the woods, following a narrow path studded with white pebbles and shells someone had collected from the shore. Sappho looked up to see the dark towering cedars brush the dome of the blue sky. Around them were salal, ferns like swords and ferns like lace, rotting mossy logs dotted with fungus. Kate picked some licorice root and passed it around ("*natural* candy, children"). It did taste a bit like licorice. On they went. As they walked deep in the cedars, the highway noise began to make itself heard. The ferry traffic was like a swift tide, rising every couple of hours and then falling back. They passed a half-finished, neglected geodesic dome. They passed through a clearing where rows of vegetables were flourishing ("the communal garden," explained Billy. "I never should've planted so much zucchini.") The forest waxed and waned again, becoming another clearing. Here stood an extraordinary kind of cabin. As they approached, two grey geese came hissing toward them, wings half-spread—guard geese, Billy said, holding them off with his stick. The geese retreated a bit.

Though small, the cabin featured two towers topped with spires. It had stained-glass windows, one on either side of the arched doorway. The arch was carved with sinuous patterns painted in glowing colours. Sappho held her breath, captivated.

Abruptly the door flew open. Through the spangled doorway sailed a pair of heavy leather workboots. The big boots landed with a loud thump-thump, sending up a cloud of dust and narrowly missing Finn. A pair of jeans with a big belt attached came next. They heard a yell. "Jeez, lady! What d'ya think—"

Now Nancy's voice could be heard rising, shrill and furious. "Get—" (a pair of woolly socks made a fluttery exit) "your disgusting *crap*" (a flannel workshirt took its leave) "out of my house!"

A lot of hippies didn't bother with underwear, Sappho surmised, because there were no underwear on the ground, and the man who now came staggering out was buck naked. His springy black head of hair was dripping with something— beer? He was carrying a big leather purse-type thing. Nancy appeared in the doorway, her face coldly furious. She wore a gauzy Indian skirt, and her arms were folded resentfully over her bare breasts.

Billy helped the naked man collect his stuff. The man— he had a bushy black beard and generous help-ings of body hair, even on his back— gathered his clothes under one arm and set off down the path, pursued by the geese. "Bye, Nancy," he muttered as he went. *"Dammit."*

"My NAME is *GALADRIEL*, you MORON!"

Billy took Finn firmly by the hand, pivoted on his heel, and walked back off towards Chickenland. Kate made a few hesitant noises, but followed, holding Sappho tightly by the hand. They heard the door slam shut. No-one looked back.

That night Finn slept up in the loft with Sappho. Billy set him up with a little cot and a sleeping bag lined with duck-hunting scenes in flannel. Sappho read to him from *The Hobbit,* and he seemed to enjoy that. Once Kate came up to snuff out the kerosene lamps, they lay in the darkness listening to the grownups whisper below. At least Sappho did, for eventually Finn's slightly ragged breathing regularized. He was asleep.

It was hard to make out exactly what they were saying, but Sappho sharpened her ears. "Total WITCH": that was Billy. "Now, Billy, you know how I feel about that word": that was Kate, murmuring on about women's wisdom and herbs and persecution. "Witless BITCH": Billy again, undaunted. "Freely expressing her sexual desires...?" Also Kate. "Oh," groaned Billy loudly, "will someone please KILL ME NOW and put me out of my misery?" And on it went. Somehow, eventually, Bilbo and Gandalf got mixed up in all this. Gandalf was saying that the Fair Folk had ways that mortal men could never make head nor tail of, and Bilbo, who was usually very respectful to the old wizard, told him to take a long walk off a short pier. It seemed to Sappho that the Ring had made Bilbo Baggins awfully cocky— after all, what did he know about the ways of the elves, really? And then Sappho was awoken by a familiar sense of foreboding. The house was silent, the grownups gently snoring.

But it was time for a trip to the outhouse.

"Use the chamberpot, dear! Honestly," Kate would often sigh, hearing her daughter struggling down from the loft in the blackness. "That's what the early settlers would've done." However much she hated creeping off to the outhouse at night, Sappho could not face the chamberpot solution.

It was difficult to make it down the rope ladder in the dark. She would have to pass Billy and Kathleen, wreathed in their fug of pungent grown-up air. Billy lay spooned behind Kate, one hand at her waist. Outside Sappho would hold her flannel nightie up so it wouldn't get wet or torn or tangled in the thorny brambles which snaked through the long grass at the sides of the path, swiping at her legs like big cats from their cages. The narrow plank was slick with moisture of one kind or another, and Sappho was afraid she would slip and fall into the ditch below. The flashlight helped a little. She hated sitting on the makeshift toilet, imagining labyrinthine passages below the earth, and shapeshifting creatures sneaking around beneath, rearing upwards; she couldn't wait to get back. Night or day, toilet paper was always damp and mildewed in the outhouse and the pages of the *Whole Earth Catalogue* someone had put there were stuck together. And when the wet weather approached with fall, the trip to the outhouse became more and more treacherous.

Finn was staying at Chickenland again, and that day, Bath Day, was a little chilly. Kate had been heating water in a huge metal pot on the wood-stove all afternoon. The kids were sharing a Mason jar of preserves—blackberries labeled Summer of '74— and were poring over Billy's collection of *Fabulous Furry Freak Brothers* comics. There was something weird about Fat Freddy's cat, thought Sappho. Oh—it had a big nose like a person. Kate was taking a damp rag to Finn's purpled lips and cheeks when all at once his mother came striding into the clearing. It was the first time Sappho had ever seen Nancy fully clothed. She was wearing a long purple dress with an elaborately embroidered bodice, together with a turquoise necklace which showed off her long neck. Her pale red hair was braided carefully and looped around her ears. Billy was off digging the midden with Dan Joe, his friend from the Rez, as was his habit most days. This left Kate to cope with the Elf Queen, who gave the most perfunctory of knocks before letting herself into the cabin, paying no mind to the rooster who had followed her through the door. Finn was crouching under the kitchen table, and Sappho crawled under to join him there.

Nancy's voice had a strained smile in it. "Kate! Haven't *you* made a difference to this old bear's den! And you've been here *such* a short time. Here, I brought you some dried herbs from my garden. They make a wonderful tea."

"Well...thank you," Kate replied uncertainly, shooing the resentful rooster out and shutting the door. "Would you... shall I make us some of it now?"

"Oh, not for me. This is more like... Kate's special blend. Has Billy still got some of that Red Zinger around?" Nancy began rummaging expertly through the cupboards.

"Have a seat, please, no really... I'll get it," said Kate. Finally Nancy tore herself away from the cabinets and sat at the kitchen table. The children shrank away from her sandaled feet.

"Fee fo fi fum! I smell the blood of someone young," said Nancy with forced jollity. "Glorfindel, I know that's you under there. Look, will you run along outside and let me talk to Kate?" Finn scrambled out on his hands and knees, making for the door, while Sappho followed.

The children spent the next hour or so dealing with the chickens. For a while they searched for eggs, and found a few under the A-frame, caked in mud and straw that looked salvageable. They sprinkled some grain around, which brought the whole flock running. Every so often the children heard noises from inside the house, and they pricked up their ears. The voices were intense, then jubilant. After a bit they heard the rumble of Billy's pickup truck approaching, gearing up for the last steep stretch of the driveway.

Apparently the women heard that too, for just as the truck pulled up, Nancy opened the door and leaned comfortably on the door-frame, smiling a wide smile. Kate hovered behind her.

"Billy... welcome home, sweetie! " said Kate brightly. "Look who's here." Sappho noticed that her mother didn't choose a name for their visitor. "She brought me some special tea."

Billy gave the boy a brief, hard hug. He went into the chicken coop without a word to the women.

Nancy rolled her eyes at Kate. "Men are such children," she said. "Come on, man-child, it's time to come home," she said, to Finn.

Finn just stared at the ground. "I was going to have a bath," he said.

"Glorfindel— *enough*, all right? Let's go." And then, as if her son had simply run away from home, "I've spent enough of my sacred energies worrying about you."

Nancy draped an arm around Kate's shoulder. "It's

been amazing, my sister. Until the next time— don't let that Leo man burn off your precious Pisces reserves!" Kate laughed a little, blushing nervously, and watched their neighbour firmly take her son by the hand and pull his pale narrow form stumbling down the path.

"Bye, Finn," Sappho managed to call out, even as the evergreens erased him.

So Bath Day proceeded without Finn. Actually, it was Bath Evening now, since it took hours to heat enough water on the woodstove to fill the huge pail they used when the weather cooled. Sappho bowed her head while Kate shampooed it with Dr. Bonner's all-purpose castile soap, squeezing her eyes shut as her mother poured pitchers of warm water through her hair. When it was squeaky, she stood while one last pitcher was emptied over her body.

Later, feeling fresh, Sappho pulled on the flannel nightie. Now that her hair was dry, the time had come for Kate to comb it out. This was an ordeal, since Sappho's hair tangled easily. "Look at this rat's nest!" her mother exclaimed, working away to unsnarl it. That took nearly an hour. Then it was time to get ready for bed. Kate was up in the loft, lighting the kerosene lamps. She would read aloud, of course, but from what? Probably *The Hobbit*, but Sappho made a show of going through the bookshelf anyway. There was that book again, the one about the man who might have been a pirate. Sappho pulled it out.

"Mom, who was Sir Francis Drake?"

"Well, Sapphie, he was a very dashing figure, an explorer from the time of Shakespeare and Queen Elizabeth the First. Queen Elizabeth sent him out on his greatest mission in the 1570s, just about four hundred years ago now. I picture someone with a goatee and tall leather boots and a big blousy white pirate shirt—"

"*Was* he a pirate? Because it says here on this book that—"

Billy joined in the conversation from below at this point. "Drake preferred the term 'privateer,'" he laughed. "But the Spanish sure as heck called him a pirate! He pillaged their ships down one side of the Americas and up the other."

"He was the first man to circumnavigate the globe," said Kate.

"What's that mean, Mom?"

"Sail all the way around it, darling."

"Which was a helluva thing to manage in those days! No Panama Canal back then, for one thing. Those sailors, they went all the way down around the tip of South America. Then they came up, Spanish and English and all, fighting each other and the elements all the way, with only their rough navigational gizmos and the starscapes to guide them. Lotta sea monsters of all types, and a lotta mermaids, reported by both sides. Drake kept looting Spanish silver and gold. The Spanish dreamed that the whole north coast was stuffed with silver—Silverado, you might say. They made up a beautiful map of the North Coast as Silverado. That hadta've spurred Drake on to keep going north, that plus looking for the fabled Northwest Passage that would bring him and his men safely and easily back to the Old World."

Sappho rested her chin on her fists. "Did he find the Northwest Passage?"

"Nope, because a safe, easy route back only really existed in his imagination. But some folks say he came all the way up here to British Columbia looking for it. To Gray Star—'cept it wasn't called Gray Star then, of course."

Kate spoke doubtfully. "Sir Francis Drake in British Columbia? I don't know, Billy... I learned he only went as far as Northern California."

"Renamed the whole coast New Albion, claimed it for his Virgin Queen. There's a dig just over the U.S. border that's turnin' up all kinds of stuff. It's at an old Makah village on Cape Flattery named Ozette. Mudslide in the 16th century wiped out the village and preserved everything, including some European coins and trinkets. Hadta've been Drake. And, if I'm right, our man sailed up past Cape Flattery to Vancouver Island and on into the Strait. Probably thought it was the Northwest Passage. Traded with the locals."

"There's nothing remotely like that in the history books, Billy. I took a course in third year..."

They could hear Billy climbing the rope ladder. They saw his fluffy yellow head pop into view. "If it were already in the history books, baby, I wouldn't have a PhD thesis worth crap. What do you think brought me up here from sunny California?"

"The war in Vietnam...?"

Billy laughed. "Hell, woman! I put in my army time ten years ago. Nah, what brought me here was my burnin', unquenchable desire to become *Doctor* Billy Black. And Berkeley gave me a big scholarship based on my Drake theory. The Museum wants coins, trinkets—tangible proof that Sir Francis Drake sailed into Georgia Strait. And I aim to give 'em what they want. Can't go back empty-handed. So until I find Drake.... You-all are stuck with me." The head ducked away.

It was Sappho's deepest wish that she and her mother would be stuck with Billy forever. Loving Billy as she did, Sappho did not know *what* to wish for.

The next time they saw Finn—about a week later— his mother had pressed him into service as a supporting player in a sunny tableau. Nancy was striding across the clearing, the wind whirling her strawberry hair around her smiling face and sending her long purple muslin dress whipping like a flag. With one hand she drew her son along; with the other, a skinny man in a black cowboy hat and a Mr. Natural ("Keep on Truckin'") t-shirt, a man who blinked in the sunlight like a mole.

"Why, if it ain't Cowboy Cal!" yelled Billy, emerging onto the porch with a coffee cup. "And the fair lady Nancy."

"How many times do I have to tell you, Billy?" replied the fair lady. "My name is Galadriel."

Kate, smiling, called her daughter down from the loft. Then all of them—Sappho, Kate, Billy, Finn, Nancy, and Cowboy Cal—sat down around the cedar table, sending a startled red hen popping out with a sharp cluck of disapproval. ("Darn it, Maybelle, scat! Isn't your coop fancy enough for you?")

Kate was pouring out coffee for some and juice for others ("Just hot water and lemon for me, please," said Nancy in an exceedingly soft voice), and Billy was teasing Cal. "Hey, man, sit down and relax. Take off your hat!" he said, reaching for it —but Cal's hands intercepted his, flying to the wide brim and yanking the hat down tightly. Billy giggled. "I barely recognize you outside your natural habitat! You're like a miner, man. Your skin's so white it's blue." Cowboy Cal was smiling, but he looked shy. Nancy was stroking his calloused and tobacco-yellowed fingers. She held them close to her face, as though she might put them in her mouth any second.

"Cal works *hard*, yeah," she dimpled. "He's saving up for something *special*." Sappho could tell Nancy meant something for her, a big present.

"Yeah, you been workin' that coffee can for a few years now. You got buried treasure?" asked Billy. "No, don't answer that. But don't let it get around the Saloon, you know what I mean?" Cal nodded solemnly, his eyes darting in all directions. Billy laughed again and gave him a long look. "Somethin' special, huh? Somethin' Nancy here oughtta like?"

Cal nodded timidly: "I think so. I'm goin' into Town" (this meant Vancouver) "for a few days next week."

"Yeah," Billy went on. "Then you two can take a holiday—get a tan at the fabulous StrarSpray Motel—just a few feet from fabulous Sandy Beach!"

Nancy grinned and frowned simultaneously, grabbing Cal's arm and pulling him close. "And Glorfindel can call him Daddy..." Nancy stage-whispered. She clutched Cal, but never once did she lift her eyes from capering Billy. Finn looked down a lot, his face smooth, expressionless.

Later, when the others were gone, Billy relaxed on the couch with a girl under either arm; Kate, Billy, and Sappho stared into the fire. Battery-operated radio played CBC FM faintly. It was a live jazz performance, with audience members breaking into applause at what seemed to Sappho like completely random moments.

"Cowboy Cal," said Kate with studied neutrality.

"Yep. Well, when seven a.m. rolls around at the ol' Goon Saloon, I guess sometimes Cowboy Cal's the only game in town." Kate took a tired swipe at him, stifling laughter, and they started some talentless wrestling.

"Could we kidnap Finn?" asked Sappho. The question froze them, and they stared at her wordlessly. Some moments passed. Then, just as Billy opened his mouth to reply, a mechanical wailing, some distance off, reached their ears—it started low and grew louder, rising and falling in waves.

"What on earth is that?" Kate asked.

"Fire drill, girls. I gotta go," said Billy, flying into action. He pulled on a heavy pair of rubber boots and a thick rain-slicker. He hugged them quickly and made for the door. They heard the truck chugging down the drive. The siren wailed on and on.

Chapter Three

Sappho had been attending Gray Star Elementary for about a year, and did not often resist going to school.

She liked grade five schoolwork: she liked her teacher, her projects on things like Mexico and the solar system, its planets hanging like fruits on an invisible tree, and books like the one on the underground *World of Og* by Pierre Berton. She didn't like the school bus, and she hated gym class. But usually she didn't mind going to Gray Star Elementary.

That damp April day was different. Sappho was halfway down the overgrown path to the highway, dimly aware of the rise in ferry traffic tide, when she realized with a lurch in her stomach that something bad was going to happen to her mother. Dropping her bookbag and her lunchbox in the bracken she turned and ran back— along the narrow path to the cedar A-frame, the chicken coop and dark evergreens and more bracken and sword ferns which slashed at her legs as she pushed by. Occasionally she had to jump to miss a speckled yellow banana slug daubed across the path, slick trail in wet leaves and water-beaded grass. By the time she saw the A-frame among the dark trees her lungs ached and burned with effort, but she managed to squeeze out a strangled "Mom! Mom!" any-way. This brought her mother gliding out on the porch, her arms and hands folded across her stomach and the red chickens skirmishing and clucking ominously. As Sappho charged up the steps the chickens exploded, shrieking and leaping in all directions.

"What is it? What is *wrong*?" said her mother, bend-ing down to embrace the girl.

Sappho flung her arms around Kathleen. Some kind of scented oil infused her long brown combed-up hair. "I can't go," she wheezed.

"Why? Why on earth not?"

"I can't leave you. I just feel like something's going to happen,"

"Like what? Don't be silly!"

"Something bad. I don't know..."

"Look. *Darling*." She crouched and looked into her daughter's wet eyes. "I'll be *fine*. I'm just going start sew-ing clothes for the Renaissance Fayre! Now go on, or you'll miss the bus."

"No, Mom. I..."

Kathleen was getting testy. "Now go *on*! This is just

silly. You are ten years old! Too big for this stuff now. Everything will be just *fine*."

Sappho relaxed her grip, giving up. Sensing this, Kathleen pressed on: "I'm going to have a nice day. I'll have some zucchini bread a woman friend brought from her freezer and finally try some of that tea our neighbour brought us, and then I'm going to work on a dress." Kate crouched down and cupped Sappho's jaw, gazing into her wet speckled eyes. "We're so lucky to be here, Sappho, in a real community, with neighbours who care about us. Now you have to dash, or you'll miss the bus. Have a good day at school!"

Sappho ran back down the path, faster now. The school bus might be there already. She whipped through the forest, grabbed her things, narrowly missed slipping on another long oozy banana slug, its tiny horns waving. Planted dolefully at the trailhead was their white VW van, slumped and staring sightlessly into the dark of the cedars, a toolbox at its side. It was a long steep run down from that point. When she burst out at the highway the yellow bus was still there, swallowing up the chubby Boley kids from across the highway. She could hear the big and baleful Boley family dog barking doomily in his pen. Wuf. Wuf. Pause. Wuf. She stepped up, out of the cool fresh air and into the stuffy bus.

Inside was a boiling, surging crowd of schoolgoers—

the usual scene, in fact. Half the kids were screaming. The other half were cringing and staring into their laps. Objects were hurtling around the bus— a whirling asteroid storm of books, toques, sandwiches, fruit. It was steamy hot in the bus, yet every kid was bundled up and zipped tight to the chin in puffy ski-jackets. French Canadian Claude was eating some little boy's lunch. One kid in a maple-leaf balaclava was choking another kid with a woolly red scarf and Canucks toque. Someone clouted someone else in the head with a sneaker. Every few minutes the driver bellowed out a command ("SHUT. UP!") which brought a microsecond of quiet before the tempest erupted with fresh fury. Only Michael Joe was oblivious, calmly staring out the window. Michael, a thin lank-haired kid from the Rez, barely acknowledged their existence. The shoes and books and lunchbox items whirled around but left him miraculously untouched.

Sappho shut her eyes and wished— hard— that she was back in the city. Before Vancouver, they had lived in New York, where Sappho had gone to Grades One, Two and Three while her mother worked in the theatre making costumes for Shakespeare plays and stuff.

Before that they had lived in London, England: there were photographs of her handsome dark-haired father, a hazy memory (a photograph?), in black pointy Chelsea boots crouched over her pram. He had been an actor.

In London, where, although Sappho could only strain to remember it, she had once held hands with Ringo Starr. Kate liked to say they were gypsies, wandering here and there. "We lived in Bayswater when you were little," she had said sometimes as they lay snuggled up in bed. "We lived in an 18th century flat with tiny little doorways, so low your father had to stoop to get through them. The landlady said the flat had belonged to one of the mistresses of a dissolute Prince of Wales. I worked so hard on that place, painting and decorating... and the people upstairs, who had a girl your age, well, they were friends with one of the Beatles. You used to go up there and play all the time. One afternoon you were up there playing with the little girl, Miranda when a knock came at our door. When I opened it, there was Ringo Starr holding you by the hand! You were three. And he said, (her mother's voice deepening to Liverpudlian) 'I believe this is your little girl, Madam?' The Beatles! And you were smiling and having a *great* time..."

WHAM! A packet of carrot sticks caught Sappho squarely on the ear. She had known the exciting streets of New York City, alive with people. She had lived in London, England, once upon a time. And now she was here. In Gray Star. Sappho rubbed her ear and looked out the window, watching the dark ranks of trees roll past, a thick impenetrable army running deep, as far back as eyes could see.

They had a brand new teacher, the last one having left to have a baby. Mr. Mahoney, nervous and woolly-vested, wore thick brown corduroy trousers and fisherman's socks with sandals. He had brown hair and a reddish moustache. Mr. Mahoney was doing the attendance. When he came to Sappho's name he smiled a knowing little half-smile which made the creatures swirl in her guts. Because she knew what that smile meant. "Smith, *Sappho*. Sappho Smith?" Mr. Mahoney raised his friendly innocent face, and she gave a weak little wave. Mr. Mahoney's gentle chestnut eyes rested on Sappho. "When I was in university I majored in literature. We read the poems of Sappho. Well, the fragments that remain." She willed the teacher to let it drop. He didn't. "I guess you haven't read them yet." She shook her head. "I guess your parents have, though." She nodded helplessly. "Wow. I would *really* like to meet your parents."

Mr. Mahoney beamed with good intentions. "Class," he said, looking around the room, "Sappho here is named for a great lyric poetess of ancient Greece. She was a great poetess and also, they say... a great... a great lover of women. She and her admirers were devoted to Aphrodite, the goddess of love and beauty. They lived on the island of Lesbos, which is actually where we get the modern word...um, *lesbian*." Mr. Mahoney carefully wrote the word LESBOS on the blackboard. He looked at the class. Not a sound. Not a snicker, not yet. The children were dumb with pleasure at this sudden windfall. Claude looked sideways at his twin, Gilles, and hoisted his thumb. "Guy La*Fleur*," Claude mouthed silently, giving thanks to his hockey god.

"Greek poetry, Mr. Mahoney?" said Gilles with an earnest little frown, leaning back and folding his arms across his Fonzie t-shirt. "Now *that* sounds cool. Guy. La. FLEUR. Teach us about Greek poetry!" A happy little pink flush tinged Mr. Mahoney's face like a sunrise.

"Well, class, Sappho was a great writer, a great poet. Some of the ancients called her the Tenth Muse. They were highly enlightened. And I guess you could say that she was a..."

"LESBO! Hey, *Lesbo*! Lesbo Smith!" The kids in the schoolyard were exultant, still unable to believe their luck, actually dancing and shivering with joy and hugging themselves with the thrill of it. The glad tidings quickly spread down the hierarchy. Shiny little faces beamed and surged up at her; eager little fingers tugged at her purple ski jacket. "Is your mom a lesbo or what?" Sappho briefly considered quibbling, then shook her head and turned away. A festive spirit shimmered through the crowd. Sappho pushed a path through her churning schoolmates and made her way Out Back with her lunch bag. They followed her a ways, then fell back, leaping and chanting, and returned to the playground to get on with the party. It was almost as bad as the time Finn let slip the fact to his Grade One class that the grownups at Chickenland went around naked in the communal garden all summer: that bit of news had bubbled up to the Grade Fives, sixes and Sevens within minutes. Sappho thought she would never live *that* down. And now this.

She sat down heavily at the base of her tree. The cedars grew dark and dense there behind the school, and the forest stretched all the way up to the powerline, to the snowline, to the civet-cats and cougars and bears. To the Sasquatch. Sappho thought she could hear the river run. She could see Michael Joe out of the corner of one eye. He sat against his tree, smoking. The smoke rose to join the mists above, which wreathed and wound among the treetops. Michael's dark head lay against the reddish bark of the cedar. His profile was cut sharp. He was twelve, but he was in her class. Was he slow? Sappho didn't think so. He almost never spoke, so it was hard to tell. But Sappho thought that Michael probably wasn't stupid or lazy at all—his mind was elsewhere, that was all.

He sure was cool. Michael's flares were tight and high-waisted, cuffed with five inches of mud and tattered where they dragged along the ground. Everyone's flares were cuffed with mud and shredded at the edges— everyone who was cool enough to have the right pants. Michael always wore the same pair of jeans, but they were faultless. Sappho had flares, at least, though they dangled a humiliating two inches off the ground because Mom, refusing to let a perfectly good pair of jeans be shredded, had hemmed them too high. Flood-pants. And they weren't as tight as Sappho would have liked. They were high-waisted enough, and they were widelegs — but they were a bit too baggy: she could all too easily zip them up while standing. She coveted pants so tight that she would have to lie on the bed and use a coat hanger to coax the zipper up.

Ruth, who'd just come stumbling Out Back in tears again, never wore flares at all; in fact she didn't wear pants, period. She wore pleated skirts like a Grade One kid, with knee-high socks. A milky-blue tracery of veins showed on her white knees. On her high white opalescent forehead too. Dust-coloured hair curled over her shoulders, secured back from her face by a cluster of barrettes. Her parents were Jehovah's Witnesses. They wouldn't let her accept Christmas presents, much less celebrate Hallowe'en, and they had a huge stash of canned food in their basement, pineapple chunks and beets and Spam.

For the End Times. When Armageddon came. Ruth said her dad said the end was coming soon.

Sappho unpacked her lunch: a cheese sandwich whiskery with alfalfa sprouts, some raisins, some carrot sticks, a thermos she left untouched. With their sour-milk smell, thermoses were gross. Ruth, her sobs ebbing into sniffles, goggled at the food. "What is that *grass* in your sandwich?" she asked. "Sprouts," replied Sappho. Her mom grew them in a jar on top of the fridge. She made her own yoghurt as well. "They're supposed to be healthy," Sappho added tonelessly.

"Ew," said Ruth.

Michael said nothing. He blew a smoke ring. Ruth asked him where his lunch was. There was a silence.

"Traded it for smokes," he said. Michael flicked a butt into a big puddle. It floated briefly and then sank.

That afternoon the class watched a movie called *The Last Spike,* which was about the cross-Canada railroad and how they built it through the Rockies and on to Vancouver. "Psst! Lesbo!" Claude was nudging her in the ribs. Sappho glared at him mutely. "Hey," he continued in a conversational kind of way, "how come you eat da grass for lunch? Are you a cow?"

When the bell rang a few grade twos ran up to tell her that some hippie was asking for her outside. Sappho went out and found Billy waiting by the chain-link fence.

His furry blond eyebrows had an anxious lift to them. "Sappho darlin', don't worry, but your mom's in the hospital," he said. Her stomach tightened. Billy's blue eyes had tears in them. Her throat tightened. "She's okay, but she had a car accident, and she's gonna be in hospital overnight. But she's ok. She's ok. The doctor doesn't know if the... but *she's* all right. She's just gotta rest."

As they drove, Billy explained. "After her tea, your mom decided to go to the General Store for groceries. And as she was getting into the van, she had stomach cramps real bad. She was worried about the... her stomach hurt real bad, so she decided to drive to Gray Star General and see a doctor. So she drove down towards the highway, and suddenly she noticed there were no brakes! No goddamn... Jesus. She had to swing hard to the right or she might've crashed into someone when she hit the highway. She swung right and flipped it right over into the ditch! I could hear her screaming clear over at Chickenland. But she's not hurt too bad. She's ok. We don't know if the baby... but your mom is in one piece, and that's the main thing."

"Baby?"

"Well, yeah. We were waiting to tell ya, but ... your mom is gonna have my baby. As long as everything's... I guess it's a lot to take in all at once."

"Billy."

"Yeah, kid?"

"You... you said you..."

"What?"

It was hard to put into words. "You said when you find Sir Francis Drake..."

He turned to look at her. "What? That I'm goin' back to California?" She nodded. "Damn, I am such an asshole. Listen: WE are goin' to California. As a family. Okay?" She nodded hard, eyes stinging. "But first we gotta find evidence Drake was here. We've been diggin' the midden for ages... but, anyway, once I'm DOCTOR Black—" he spun the steering wheel hard right, and the truck chugged up the road to Gray Star General—"I can tie the knot with your mom and be Daddy Black too."

Sappho felt hope rush through her.

"I should've gotten rid of that van a long time ago," said Kate, paler than her milky blue hospital gown. Her long brown hair spread out on the pillow. Kate reached a limp arm out from the white bed. The other arm was snaked with tubing. "It was already a wreck when we drove it across Canada. What a *disaster!* I wound up upside-down with my ankle caught in the door. I thought my foot might be cut off; I couldn't feel a thing below my knee! I was yelling and screaming. Luckily, Billy heard over at the chicken coop."

Billy affirmed this.

"I told them: I. NEVER. Want to see that van again! I said— *take it away!*" Sitting up straight in bed, Kathleen made a grand sweeping gesture and pointed imperiously into the distance. She kept talking about the van—how it had got them through the Rockies and across the province only to break down near Hell's Gate, how they had spent a week in Hope, B.C., waiting for the mechanic to get back from his honeymoon. It seemed to Sappho that her mother, by talking on, louder and faster, was drowning out other voices.

Finally Kate sank back into the pillows and smiled wearily. "So I'm stuck here for a bit. But you two will be fine. Someone from the Sisterhood will be over with dinner and good vibes! My friends promised they'd organize it. Someone'll be there when you get home, you'll see." She leaned back smiling peacefully. Billy grumbled something inaudible.

They came home to find that the Sisters were as good as their word. Nancy sitting at their kitchen table, her hair lit up fiery by the kerosene lamp. Finn was curled up in the window seat, reading. "Soup's on," she sang out in her little-girl voice. "You two must be hungry."

Billy stopped, looked at her blankly. "Soup now is it? Don't do us any more favours, all right? Keep your 'herbal tea' to yourself in future."

"Just what are you insinuating, Billy Black?" Nancy shot back, her voice higher than ever, and tremulous.

"Just LEAVE my lady-friend alone. No more cute little gifts."

"Typical male chauvinist crap! It makes you nervous when we women make a connection."

"You know what makes me nervous, *Nancy*? YOU do, period."

He went out to minister to the chickens.

Sappho saw Nancy make a willful effort to calm herself. After a few minutes, she lowered her pale kohl-rimmed eyes at Sappho and patted the seat beside her. "Billy and his macho head-trips, huh?" she said, blue eyes rolling. She squeezed Sappho's hand. "Girls together."

Girls together: it didn't last long. Nancy had made an elaborate supper, and began, with little hums and balletic flourishes, setting the table for four. She laid out the casserole and the pie. She jangled the cowbell from the porch. No Billy. The crockery sat cooling on the tatted tablecloth while the kids sat on the sofa, stomachs rumbling. They hit the floor when Nancy abruptly threw the soup tureen across the room in the general direction of the chicken coop, smashing a window. She yanked the now-crying Finn by his arm and marched him out the door, down the stairs and out into the black. "Leave him here, leave him," sobbed Sappho, on and on until Finn's moans were inaudible.

Billy came back.

He picked her up and hugged her, jogging her on one hip as if she were three. "Lord," Billy murmured, looking at the shard-scattered room.

He looked at Sappho with some kind of apology in his eyes. "I know, I know: kidnap, eh? You figure we stick a black wig on him or somethin'? He'd look like that kid from *The Jungle Book.* "

"Mowgli."

In the end, they didn't need to disguise Finn as Mowgli in order to bring him back to Chickenland to stay. The ball got rolling the next night. It was a Saturday. Finn appeared at the cabin door at dusk. Sappho was up in the loft using her felt pen set to draw a magic horse when she heard him come in. No-one else was there: Kate was still at the hospital, keeping quiet to keep the baby, and Billy was off somewhere—probably at the dig. Sappho let her head dangle over the edge, and motioned for Finn to climb up. His arm was starting to bruise. For a while they just lay in bed with the covers pulled up snug; Sappho showed him her horse drawing and added a second, slightly smaller horse for him. "Put wings," he whispered. She added wings and lots of detail to the feathers.

The late afternoon light deepened through gold to orange and began evaporating. It was time to light the kerosene wicks, so they did. Then they made some peanut butter and honey sandwiches. "Are you still hungry, Finn? I am."

"Billy says when we're hungry we can always go hunting for eggs," observed Finn loyally. Eggs were hidden all over Chickenland, as if for some perpetual Easter morning hunt. "Or we can find licorice root in the forest."

"Let's go to the Goon Saloon," Sappho said suddenly.

"My mom says I'm not allowed."

So what? Who cares what she says? Where is she, anyhow?"

"At the Goon Saloon, I guess."

"Well, I heard at school that place is against the law anyways. So if it's against the law in the first place, grown-ups can't make up other rules about it," Sappho reasoned.

Finn stared at her.

"C'mon, we'll sneak down there," urged Sappho. "We'll spy. It'll be fun."

Finn looked more pliable.

"I bet there's junk food at the Goon Saloon," Sappho said thoughtfully. "I bet there's pop and chips." Privately, she doubted this. But Finn fell for it.

"Yah! Pop and chips!" he cried. "Let's go!" They bent down to tie extra knots in their North Stars. Sappho grabbed a flashlight, and out they went, hand-in-hand, into the darkening forest.

Reaching the highway, they faced the oncoming traffic—rising now, for the seven-ten had docked a few minutes before—and stuck out their thumbs. It wasn't long before Dan Joe pulled over in a rusted-out 1969 Pontiac. They ran up to meet him, opened the front door and clambered in.

"We're headed down to the General Store, please," said Sappho. The good thing about Dan Joe was that he never posed any questions. The General Store closed at six, as everyone knew. But Dan Joe didn't say a word. He just drove on in silence. Dropping them at their destination, Dan Joe gazed at them incuriously for a moment. Thanking him (no reply), Finn and Sappho hopped out and ambled over to the store, where they sat on the steps until the Pontiac had disappeared around the bend.

They sat and stared at the abandoned store-front across the road. Above it was the Goon Saloon. A few cars were parked near the stairs. Music and several voices could be heard.

Too scared to budge, Sappho and Finn stayed where they were.

Bob's black lab ambled over and lay at their feet with a sigh. A banty rooster and five banty hens darted purposefully by. The sound of laughter issued from the open windows of the Goon Saloon.

After a while, a truck, old but brightly painted with rainbows, pulled up. It was Cal's. Cal and Nancy emerged. They looked dressed up: Cal wore a new cowboy hat with a beaded band and a leather vest. Nancy wore a voluminous aqua-blue gown embroidered with butterflies. Her eyes were dark with kohl and mascara. They linked arms. "We're steppin' out, babe!" Cal declared.

"Mom!" called Finn. She turned.

"What are you kids doing here? You know this place is for adults. We come here for a *break*."

"Ah, well," said Cal, "let's run 'em back."

"Crap! I want to have a good time. Right. Now!" squeaked Nancy. She propped her fists on her hips and stamped her foot. "No. I won't have my evening ruined. We're going in. They're coming too."

"But, babe—"

"Don't 'babe' me! What difference does it make? If they want to see the place so badly, let them see it. But they'd better not get in the way," Nancy added, taking Finn's elbow with one hand and Sappho's with the other. Radiating impatience, she marched them up the stairs.

The patrons of the Goon Saloon didn't take much notice of Sappho and Finn. They were too busy passing one big joint after another around the room. Sappho thought that the pot smelled like smoked fish. Nancy steered the kids to a big booth off to one side and went up to the long cedar bar. Cowboy Cal took out his guitar and began tuning up. A moment later the bushy-haired waitress, Maureen, came and dropped a heavy pottery bowl in front of Sappho and Finn. It was filled with raisins and sunflower seeds— not junk food at all (that had been a longshot), but they gulped it down fast.

The room was getting noisier and hazier. People were coming in all the time. Motorcycles roared outside. Up the stairs and into the Goon Saloon clumped three huge men with long beards. They wore weather-beaten black leather jackets with skull-and-crossbones insignia on the backs. Looking over at Sappho, one said something to his companions, and they all three exploded with laughter. ("I think those are pirates," whispered Finn. "Like in Tintin.") One of them got up from his barstool and lumbered over to their table, where he leaned in close, his reddened eyes raking over her. "Not quite ripe, are ya, jailbait?" he said, breathing sickly-sweet fumes into her face. "But it won't be long now..." he added, reaching over with a big hand tattooed L-O-V-E. Finn reared up on the seat and hissed like a goose, craning his neck and spreading his arms like wings. Maureen began running interference, distracting the pirate with more booze. He stumbled back to his companions, waving his drink.

Nancy buzzed around chatting rapidly to regulars, taking no notice of Sappho and Finn. She disappeared for a few minutes. Then she rematerialized and slid into an armchair across the room, where she leaned back, clutching a bottle. Nancy was watching Cowboy Cal, perched with his steel-string on a stool in the centre of the Goon Saloon. Nancy guzzled liquor, exposing her white throat. She toyed with her turquoise beads.

"This one's a Dylan tune," said Cal, prodding howls of appreciation from the patrons. "It's goin' out to my special lady-friend. The song's called 'I Want You,'" he added, fixing Nancy with a melting look as he launched into the song. Blow-Yer-Brains-Out Bob lurched over and joined in on harmonica. Nancy, swaying in time, finished the contents of her bottle and raised her hand to Maureen, who brought another.

When Cowboy Cal finished playing, Nancy gave a high-pitched hoot and swigged away. Then Cal climbed off the stool, crossed the floor and went down on one knee before her. The crowd grew quiet. "Lady Galadriel," Cal began. She smiled benevolently. Cal darted a glance up at her, flushed, and bowed his head again. "C'mon, Cal!" shouted someone near the bar. "Go for it!"

"For like two years now I been saving up my tips for something special," Cal went on. "Something special to win your favour." Nancy drew herself up straight, ready to receive tribute. "So I went to Town last week and spent all my silver. For you." With that, Cal swept his cowboy hat off to reveal his sparse scalp.

"Look careful, Galadriel! There's a little garden there," said Cal, his head still bent. Pause. The lady's face registered puzzlement and then rising annoyance.

"I got hair plugs, babe! Right now they're just like rows of seedlings, but the doc says pretty soon they'll grow up real strong. I'll have my hair back!" Sure enough, once she looked closely Sappho could see little rows of hair planted in neat lines across Cal's scalp. Her Malibu Barbie's flaxen hair hung the same way, if you inspected her rubber head closely enough.

There was silence in the Goon Saloon, as though all the revelers were afraid to draw breath. Suddenly Nancy emitted a loud furious shriek. Sappho felt Finn's thin hand grope for hers, and she clasped it tight. Nancy emptied her bottle and then threw it, sending it across the room and out the window. The bottle shattered on the street below. Reaching over the table with a wolfish smile, Nancy laid her hand on Cowboy Cal's scalp. She took hold of the hair plugs. She smiled wider and pulled hard. Cal screamed, and Finn screamed too. But his mother was past hearing, past seeing. She stood on the table, her colour high, a tiny bouquet of hair twisted between her fingers. Drawing a big breath, she let loose:

"You. Fucking. *Peacock*! How DARE you make a FOOL of me in front of all these people?! Instead of buying me something I WANT, like a RING—" she paused for a swig "you *treat yourself to hair-plugs*?!"

"I thought you'd like me better my hair back, babe! I did it for you! Oh, Lord, oh Jesus—" gibbered Cal.

"Of all the ridiculous, vain MORONS—" she shrieked, mascara running in black rivulets down her cheeks, and flung the uprooted seedlings in his face.

The Goon Saloon erupted, chairs and bottles flying from every direction. Nancy launched herself at Cowboy Cal, who was clutching his bleeding scalp and moaning. Blow-Yer-Brains-Out Bob tackled her and she hit the floor. Sappho pulled Finn under the table and wrapped her arms around him. Maureen the waitress was standing on the bar now, yelling at everyone in her hoarse way ("Cool it!"), when Officers Macleod and Stivitch came slamming through the saloon doors. They took statements from a few people. Then they arrested the still-swearing Nancy and tugged her down the stairs in handcuffs. Cowboy Cal trailed behind, imploring them all—Nancy, the police— to relent.

Billy pulled up in the truck just in time to see the RCMP cruiser pull away with Nancy in the back seat. He hopped out and started up the stairs, hollering ("Sappho!

Finn! Dammit, are you in here? Of all the Godforsaken dumps!") Hearing his voice, the children crawled out from under the table.

Billy's questions would start energetically enough, then trail off faintly. "What the hell are you kids doing in this...?" Pause. "Did that crazy-woman...?" Pause. He went over to the bar, quizzed a few bystanders, and came back with two bottles of Coke and trailing Cowboy Cal.

Soon, all four of them were seated in the pickup: Billy, Finn, Sappho, and Cowboy Cal, who had bits of paper napkin stuck to his head and blotches around his eyes. "*You got the silver,*" Cal sang in a cracking whisper. "*You got the gold...*"

"We'll just pop around to Gray Star General to get you checked out, man," said Billy levelly. "We can peek in on Kate too."

And that was how Finn came to stay at Chickenland indefinitely.

Chapter Four

Sappho was up at five a.m. the morning of the school camping trip. At camp, the principal had promised, the student body of Gray Star Elementary would really learn to rough it in The Bush. On her way back from the outhouse, Sappho, nearly slipping on the mossy damp plank that bridged the ditch, remembered his speech to the assembly. "All right, you people," Mr. Wetmore had boomed from the auditorium stage. He paused, waiting for the keening of the PA system to subside. Mr. Wetmore looked like an immense Weeble—tall and portly, with tiny features gathered in the middle of his big face. He had big glasses and a brush-cut.

"Silence, people!" After five minutes of fierce shushing from the teachers, everyone simmered down. Except for the boys, who were lobbing spitballs with grenade-launcher sound effects. And the girls, nudging each other and giggling.

"The Grade Five trip to Camp Gray Star is set for next month. You will set off on April 3rd."

Muddled response: nobody quite sure how to take this.

"Silence, people. People: silence. You young people lead *lives* of *luxury*," he told them, rocking on his heels violently to punctuate key words and phrases. "But life is not always soft and cushy! In the real world, people, life is often *hard* and *rough*. This camping trip will do you all a world of good."

Sword-ferns slashed at Sappho's calves as she fought her way back to the A-frame. Under the dripping eaves, she tackled a pile of damp logs, axe in hand. Half an hour later she had chopped enough kindling to start a fire in the woodstove. The rooster began to crow, and now the hens awoke, clucking and beginning to issue from the coop, pecking at nothing. Billy and Finn were still in bed, but Sappho wanted to be ready for the camping trip. An hour later she carried a steaming bowl of porridge back to bed and huddled under the covers to eat it. A mouse loped across the mattress. It sat up on its haunches and gazed at her, unafraid.

Maybe now Mom would let her get a cat.

The Grade Fives herded onto the schoolbus with their backpacks and sleeping bags, waving to a small crowd of misty-eyed parents. A few kids had never spent nights away from home before, and there were some trembling lips. As the bus pulled away, someone started them off singing "Ninety-Nine Bottles of Beer", but they were scarcely into their third brew before the trip was over— they had reached Camp Gray Star. They pulled into the driveway, passing the implausibly colourful Indian totem pole (it didn't look much to Sappho like the totem poles Billy had showed her near the dig): a blue eagle, wings outspread, atop a crouching purple beaver atop a crimson bear atop a frog; the sea-serpent twisted from top to bottom.

Someone hopped out to open the rustic crossed two-by-fours of the gate. The bus moved down the drive through the waving cedars and pulled into a wide clearing.

The dark pendulous evergreen boughs lay well back from this clearing. Long stems of purple and white-speckled foxgloves swayed in the cool wind. Sappho saw eight small white cabins ringing a larger white house with a big stone chimney. Beyond that lay cliffs. Beyond the cliffs, gray sea met the gray horizon.

Someone was tugging at her sleeve. It was Ruth, her designated camp buddy.

"What?"

"Dibsies."

"On what?"

"Dibsies on the top bunk!" Ruth charged off towards their cabin.

There were bunk-beds with clean sheets and striped wool blankets. There were also *bathrooms*, one per cabin, with flush toilets, showers that rained hot water just like that, and newly laundered towels. Sappho shivered with gladness.

Claude and Gilles stuck their heads in. "Hey, Lesbo," said Gilles casually. "Hey, dis whole place is a dump! There's only one t.v. in da whole stupid camp. I bet we hafta miss 'Happy Days' or da Canadiens game to watch something stupid with da whole class!" They ran off.

Sappho flushed the toilet experimentally. It worked. She knew she was going to love camping.

One morning the whole class hiked out from the campground on a field trip to the river. The salmon were coming back to spawn and die, dragging their heavy carcasses against the swift current, beating a hard path back to their birthplace. Their bodies were already in an advanced state of decay: the fish were shedding scales and bleeding and losing little chunks of flesh. It was horrible, but Mr. Mahoney declared it a miracle of nature. "It's beautiful," he said, holding a clipboard to his chest. "It's part of the cycle." Everyone had to do a project on the salmon.

"Class," called the teacher. "Class. Please pay attention to the fish." The kids lined the bridge on both sides, watching the fish, some— like Claude and Gilles— dangling perilously in mock fascination. The smell of dying fish-flesh was inescapable.

"Class, the fish you see were born right here. They swam out as young fish, and instinct has driven them back up this particular river. Against the tide— Claude, Gilles, will you please stop that— against the tide, against the current, against all odds they have returned to their birthplace. To spawn and to die." Horrible, horrible. The river was cloudy with blood, and bits of fish meat scattered and rode back to the sea.

Timidly Mr. Mahoney asked Michael Joe whether he could explain the return of the fish in Native terms. "Can you tell us the tale of the Salmon People, Michael?"

"Nope," said Michael Joe. He could not.

"Well, I respect that. I hope you don't mind if I try, though ..." the teacher stuttered, and, getting no response from Michael Joe beyond a tiny shrug, he began telling a story about a Salmon Princess who dwelt in the river, left her treasure there, swam out to the wilderness of the ocean, and found herself compelled back again. Following the stars, she made her way back. She swam deep down to the riverbed and beyond, down into tunnels and caves, seeking the treasure. The children weren't paying much attention. Mr. Mahoney blushed and stuttered again.

A shout rose up as Claude's red toque fell into the river, and Mr. Mahoney, giving up on the Salmon People story, took advantage of the distraction to change the subject. Once the toque had swirled off and seemed to be gone for good, he guided his pupils back to Camp Gray Star.

Sappho got home a week later with freshly laundered clothes, humming the theme to 'Happy Days' and clutching a small totemic creature carved in cedar: they had each made one, with varying degrees of success. She had never feasted on so many hamburgers, hotdogs, and roast marshmallows.

Kate was back from the hospital. Now, hugging her mother eagerly, Sappho could feel a swell to her belly. The baby was safe. "I didn't tell you right away, sweetheart, because I wanted to be sure," said Kate cautiously. "But yes—you're going to have a little brother or sister in about six months!"

"*Half*-brother or sister."

"Does that make any difference? Don't you love Billy?"

"Of course I do." Sappho did love Billy. She wanted him to be her stepfather. She pictured an unbroken circle—Kate, Billy, Sappho, the new baby, still faceless, sexless and nameless; Finn was there too. Outside the circle was a shadowed figure trying to break it all up. "Will you and Billy get married?"

Kate laughed and looked a bit vague. "Oh, I don't know... we'll see. Sometimes I think marriage is only... I mean, it certainly didn't convince your father to stay with us..."

"But, Mom..."

"What is it, Sappho?"

"I just wish..."

Sappho didn't say more: her mother's face had such a faraway cast about it. Sometimes Kate's attention wandered as if someone had turned a radio dial in her head. Now she began fingering materials—velvet, silk, suede— and all at once she was planted at the Singer sewing machine, feet on the treadle.

"What do you want to wear to the Renaissance Fayre, dear? It'll be here before we know it!"

That was how time seemed to run to adults. They always said it ran faster every year. To Sappho, a huge gulf yawned between now and July. She still had Sports Day to face before the school year ended, and that meant lots and lots of Mr. Lith's excruciating P.E. classes to endure. She knew she would never get beyond Bronze in the government's Participaction program.

Sure enough, the next morning Mr Lith, a solid blond

Swede whose sky-blue eyes were set deep under his heavy browbone, was blowing his whistle in the gym. All the girls were lined up waiting to attack the parallel bars. All except Sappho, who hung back, crossing her arms miserably over her chest. Ahead of her was Lisa, hopping up and down with so much excitement that her high shiny brown ponytail bounced violently. Her lithe frame tilted forward. Lisa bent down on one knee as though for a race. The whistle shrieked and she lunged at the twin bars, skittering on her hands, pulling her long muscled legs up so that her whole body formed a V, spinning on one hand, and topping it all off with a backwards flip. Lisa landed weightlessly and raised her arms in triumph. The class applauded. Sappho's breathing sped up.

When Mr. Lith finished smiling at Lisa he turned his icy stare on Sappho. Did his shoulders slump a little? He blew the whistle; Sappho hesitated. Mr. Lith shouted "Come on! Onto the bars!" Feeling sick, feeling her classmates' eyes upon her, Sappho took a stumbling run at the bars, tripped, and landed in a heap on the mat.

Baseball was even worse. Boys were involved. They picked the teams: their first few choices—all boys themselves— would jog lightly to the leader's side, light, strong and confident. Then came the most athletic and popular girls, smiling and nonchalant. Michael Joe was picked mid-stream. He was lean and could run and hit when he wanted to, but didn't care enough about winning to make a truly valuable player. And so on down the line, until Sappho and Ruth were left. Last, always last. As Sappho joined her team, she could see eyes rolling furiously.

The problem with baseball? The isolation. The exposure. Up to bat, Sappho cringed in the spotlight. The rival team crowed with pleasure. "Easy outer! Move in!" There were the outfielders arrayed along the baseline or closer. Once she had helped her team strike out, Sappho preferred playing outfield herself. Trying to look alert, she would will the ball away. This form of prayer didn't work very efficiently. There she would be in the full glare of the spotlight, the ball hurtling towards her from the heavens, ready to blacken her eyes, break her nose and teeth. Eyes shut tight, she usually dodged it. Her teammates' incredulous howls of frustration rang in her ears. She would be picked last for the rest of her school-days, that much was clear. Of all team sports, Sappho preferred soccer, when she could stick close to the crowd following the ball, and never feel every scornful eye upon her.

But Kate's energetic preparations for the Renaissance Fayre did hold out the promise that school and its sports activities would eventually end. Summer would arrive one day. And arrive one day it did, bringing with it Sappho's eleventh birthday and one of their long afternoons at the beach. Billy parked the truck near the banks of bright pink, fragrant wild roses and they all picked blackberries from the bushes that flourished near the seawater. Then, fingers and lips purple-stained, they made their way to the sand and spread their towels. Sappho was proud of her birthday present, a blue bikini she had picked out on a rare trip to the mall. She and Finn spent their beach afternoon floating, as usual, on logs. These logs, fugitives from the massive booms tugboated up and down the coast, lay in lines parallel to the shore. The old ones were silver with exposure to wind, rain and sun. They made great benches, picnic spots, landmarks, even hiding spots, but they were best when dragged into the sea to float.

Billy took charge of pulling the really big ones, too big for kids to manage, lugging them tirelessly up and down Sandy Beach in his frayed cutoffs. Sappho and Finn spent hours on those logs, lying to tan or feign sleep or stare at the skies, toppling off, clambering back on, paddling with their limbs; casting the logs as cruise ships, sea-serpents, dolphins. Sappho slipped off the back of her dolphin and swam to the sea-floor. She took a sea-creaturely look about her. She imagined herself as a mermaid, pressing her legs together to make a tail. How did the air-world look from the sea floor? All she could see was a circle of blue sky as her body buoyed upwards. She dove again, fanning the water, trying to stay below a bit longer. The blue disc shimmered at the edges before she broke the surface. The next time down she saw Finn close by, his brown skin bleached luminous, his white hair silvery green. He was waving his arms. Back on their tipsy log they compared wrinkled fingers.

"Hey, let's hope the Siren doesn't show up!" called Billy. Sappho hoped for the opposite. Billy always talked about creatures like the Siren, the big mermaidish monster who idled at the mouth of the river. He warned laughingly of Sasquatches who would amble down from the mountain-top and into Chickenland. Maybe they would come home to find a Sasquatch family tucked up in their beds or at the breakfast table eating porridge, he said. The Three Sasquatches. Sappho didn't tell him that Sasquatches would probably rampage through the coop, biting the heads off chickens and gulping the birds down like snack food.

Kate called them in for sandwiches and lemonade, and to get a little shade, a little rest. She didn't swim, just laid there far from the water, up near where the sand gave way to grass and yellow-flowering broom. Enjoying the hot light, Kate let the sun darken her skin. She kept squeezing lemons or home-made chamomile tea over her hair in hopes of lightening it a bit—"this is all-natural," she noted with satisfaction. She liked to spread

Johnson's baby oil on herself, rubbing lots on her preg-
nant belly. Kate didn't shave her legs or armpits. None of
the hippie mothers did. Sappho stretched out on a towel,
squinting her salty eyelashes to the precise point where
the beachscape went bejeweled with crystalline light,
and made a few plans for puberty. She would be waiting
with a Gillette razor when the hair came. Digging her feet
into the warm sand, Sappho flirted with sleep.

Later, while Finn examined the creatures in a tide-
pool, she walked along the shore, collecting shells pink
and tiny as baby's toenails and pieces of pale mint-green
glass, their edges worn smooth by the sea. A tiny island lay perhaps half-a-mile out from the beach. Sappho
pictured a castaway dropping a bottle into the water. It
broke, and the shards drifted and were worn smooth in
the tides. As for the furled message, a fish gobbled it up.

"Billy?" she called sleepily. He was stretched on a
towel beside Kate, who nudged him awake.

"Yes, kid?"

"Can we go to that island?"

"Right now? It'll take a while by log."

Giggling, Sappho poured sand on his back.

"Hey, I surrender! We can go to *Vancouver* by log if
you want. After my nap..."

They stayed at the beach through the lightshow of
sunset and on into nightfall. They built a fire and, as a

special birthday treat, roasted marshmallows. And the starscapes stretched over the sea-stars below.

Sappho, Kate, Billy and Finn got up early the day of the Fayre. It was going to be held in the forest upriver. The men had built a rustic little bridge and raised a ribboned maypole in an open glade. It wouldn't be hard to magick themselves four centuries back in time, though they would have to block out the presence of the Gray Star Golf Ground a few hundred yards away. A few hundred yards became a few hundred years and more as the Fayre-goers trickled into the forest on foot that day.

The weather was good— sunny and hot enough for them to cherish the cool of the woods and the river nearby. Artisans set up their booths on the edge of the clearing. There were potters with their heavy dark wares, weavers with colourful woolens that smelled pungently of sheep. One lady was laying out beadwork—necklaces and bracelets and other things that caught Sappho's eye. Stained glass was on offer. There was fresh produce.

One table marked FREE FOOD was stacked with speckled green zucchini, including one squash the size of a saxophone. Someone had produced mead. An array of pipes and feathered and beaded roachclips were laid out for sale. A young man in an embroidered vest strolled affably through the scene playing a mandolin and singing "Scarborough Fair." Another young man was trying to juggle.

Kate had had a hand in making many of the costumes. Sappho thought her mother's booth was the prettiest, with its carefully folded shirts, vests and dresses, some embroidered with leaves and flowers, fanned out on the table. She was proud of their matching gowns, which were pale green silk, with snug bodices and long-flowing skirts. Billy was dressed as Sir Francis Drake, pirate-style in a big blousy white shirt, a big sash and leather leggings. Finn, dressed in a similar outfit, had brought along the little Boley kid from across the highway. He gripped a chunky toy hot rod with both hands. "They didn't *have* hot rods in the Olden Days," Sappho pointed out, but the Boley kid started to cry when she tried to confiscate it ("Aw, lay off the kid, hon," said Billy). Dressing the Boley kid had been a last-minute affair, but he looked pretty happy in a grownup man's velvet tunic. Kate had gathered it in with a thick heavy leather belt drawn tight around his hips. It made playing a bit awkward, but the Boley kid looked happy. The two boys ran off ("Let's maple-leaf we're PIRATES!" "Yeah!"), slim Finn well ahead of the heavier Boley kid.

As the sun climbed higher the Fayre-ground grew hotter and noisier. "Are ya thirsty, kid?" asked Billy, feeling around in his pockets. He gave her a handful of quarters. Sappho hugged Billy and ran off to the fresh juice stand. She would have enough left over to buy a string of green glass beads.

A troupe of performers with bright-brushed hair hanging past their waists performed a maypole dance, each grasping a long satin ribbon. A lot of people were drinking mead and dabbing their temples with essential oils. Costumed children ran around laughing and dancing with the intense self-consciousness of small children in crowds, certain that everyone is watching. Gradually it grew less easy to project oneself back to the Olden Days: curiosity-seekers were arriving. Bikers roared right into the glade, and some tourists parked their Winnebago behind the glassblowers. Sound carried over from the Straight world of the golf-course too ("FORE!") and golf-carts carrying men in white or powder-blue acrylic slacks could be glimpsed. Sappho now tried to imagine that the Olden Days were being visited by time-travellers from the future. She, an innocent princess of yore, would be stunned and intrigued.

One minute the Boley kid was up on the bridge, tranquilly playing with his car while Finn was off getting his face painted. The summer sun beamed bright through the cedars, casting dappled shadows on the Boley kid's berry-pink cheeks. He had curly glossy brown hair and grubby little sugar-sticky hands. He knit his brow in con centration, paying scant attention to his surroundings, to the country fair which had brought all of Gray Star and most of the Summer People out. Sappho watched the visitors as they wandered from stand to stand, buying candles hand-dipped into rainbows of colour and doughy pottery and thick hand-woven fabrics. The Boley kid did not. One minute he was tilting his car in the dust, adding complicated sound effects, revvings and screechings and brakings. The next minute he was under the water.

How had he passed that wet threshold so silently? Sappho glimpsed him stretched out below, deep behind the window of water, his image blurry behind the current, his face turned away in profile as though listening to some distant call. She hung out over the river, her mouth open soundlessly. Her throat seemed to fill with water. But before another second passed she perceived a big figure slice past: it was Billy. Billy went into the river and snatched the Boley kid back. In seconds Billy broke the surface downstream, spluttering and sodden with his heavy package— heavy, but thankfully not limp. The boy was coughing and jerking around like a hooked fish— alive, alive. Billy hung the boy upside down and shook him, then laid him down on the grass. The Boley kid was back. He was back.

"Where's my CAR?" he managed to choke out.

"Sorry, kid," said Billy. Sappho brought his little gold-rimmed glasses from the bridge, and he put them on. "Your car's in the drink."

The Boley kid began to cry angrily. His hot salt tears slid over his cold wet cheeks and into his dripping hair. "I want my *car*."

At this point one of the Boley women appeared—an aunt? Cousin? "What the hell is going on here?" she demanded. "Mister, what did you do to this kid?"

Billy laughed. "I thought *you* at least would know his name," he said.

The Boley woman clutched the drenched and sobbing boy to her side. "Goddamn hippie!" she called at Billy's wet retreating ponytail.

⁺⁺⁺

In dreams Sappho saw it all from the other side. She saw the Boley kid playing above on the bridge through the thick wall of moving water; she saw the girl on the bridge look round idly at the fair. Beckoning to the boy from below, she called him wordlessly, and he turned and levelly met her gaze. Pushing through water to meet him she was— pushing, pushing, though instead of breaking into air and sunlight she broke the surface of the nightmare, woke up sweating in the dark. Her frightened moans found an echo in the wind. Whirling branches slapped at the window. She lay there drenched and leaking from the eyes, her heart pounding as though it would jump through her chest. Sappho lay there in her bed, wet as a swimmer.

It happened all the time now.

Chapter Five

Sappho was walking to the store. The autumn rain had been coming down hard and little rivulets coursed alongside her. Down the snaking paved road she could see a menacing group of Grade Sevens slowly working their way up the road, against the current. She would have to pass them, she knew that, unless she wanted to jump the deep watery ditch and hide in the wet bushes again, amid the salmonberry stalks and stiff salal leaves which tipped raindrops down her collar. She glanced over there, and glimpsed some dark thing float swiftly down the ditch. Well, anyway, if she ran they might see her and follow her. Sappho kept walking and they made their slow progress as well.

It was The Gang. There were five of them, two girls walking and three guys on ten-speed bikes, looping around the girls. The boys maneuvered their 10-speeds in such a way as to match the girls' slow pace without actually capsizing in the process. They were shadowed by a few irritable crows, which circled and flapped and occasionally settled on the power lines overhead, cawing gutturally. The girls' hands were nestled deep in the pockets of their short ski-jackets, their dragging feet invisible under the mud-caked wideleg Star Jeans. The boys hung over their handlebars, periodically flipping their heads back in a futile effort to keep their feathery locks in place— at a ninety-degree angle to their profiles; that was the ideal. One girl pulled her comb from a back pocket and drew it horizontally through her dark blond hair. That was Shelley. Another pulled out a pack of cigarettes and a lighter: Lisa. A cyclist, Troy—a junior hockey player, Sappho knew — wobbled and nearly toppled into the group. He swore: *crap*, man. His flares were caught in the bike-chain. He yanked the pant-leg free, and it emerged grease-blackened and torn.

Nearly there.

"Hey, Lesbo. Nice *floods*." Sappho's heart kicked against her ribcage.

"Hey, yeah. Nice flood-pants, okay?'

"Yeah, where's the flood, eh?"

She put her head down and kept walking. Big raindrops started to fall, hitting her face. The group briefly fell into her slipstream, yelling about her pants. The black birds added their croaks. Then Troy nearly toppled again, swearing extravagantly. The Gang laughed, and, forgetting the outsider girl and her shameful flood-pants, continued up the hill with the crows in tow.

Sappho went into the General Store and laid down a quarter for a bottle of Coke. She saw Ruth over by the magazine rack. Ruth darted a nervous glance her way. Holding the coveted glass bottle in two hands, Sappho walked out and huddled under the eaves. The rain was coming down hard now. Two dogs joined her there. One dog was black—Bob's dog— the other gold. They cocked their heads hopefully and slapped their meaty tails behind them. They stared with their soft brown eyes.

Ruth came out of the store carrying the October issue of *Tiger Beat* magazine. On the cover was Leif Garrett tilting his head quizzically to one side, all soft gold hair and soft brown eyes. And soft pink lips like damp heavy petals. Leif wore a choker of white pooka shells and a tight white t-shirt with "Spirit of '76" in a spray of red and blue stars emblazoned on the chest. Gold southern light hung about him, and a few blurry palms were visible in the background. Ruth leafed through the shiny pages and showed Sappho a picture of the Bay City Rollers posing jauntily in their plaid flares. Flood pants, actually, though somehow they got away with this and nobody complained.

Ruth asked Sappho which one she thought was the cutest. "None of them are as cute as Leif Garrett," replied Sappho. Actually, none of them were particularly cute, period. Woody was probably the ugliest, with his buck teeth fighting to escape a narrow palate. The most noticeable was Eric, who had the biggest and airiest shag and wore a lot of silvery-blue eye shadow. His big heavy-lidded knowing eyes tilted downwards. "Everyone says Eric is a fag," observed Ruth. This was true. Everyone did solemnly say that, all the time: Eric is a faggot. It was the eyeshadow.

"Could you keep this for me?" asked Ruth, holding out the magazine. "I'm not allowed to get stuff like this."

"Me either." Mom thought magazines like *Tiger Beat* were as bad as junk food. And she thought junk food was really bad. ("I won't have that commercialist garbage in our place!")

"But you won't get in *trouble*. Your mom is nice," wheedled Ruth. "Come on, please? Pretty please?"

"Pretty please with sugar on top?"

Ruth nodded so hard that her hair-bow slipped off.

Sappho said she would hide the *Tiger Beat* under her bed. "I'm gonna read it," she warned. "But I won't open the poster." Ruth skipped around, singing a little song of delight.

Sappho had been huddling on the porch of the General Store for a little while when Billy screeched up in his truck, a rusted farm relic from the Depression which he had rescued from the wreckers. He leaped out, swearing. "That *f—jerk*," he said, stabbing his index finger at a slowly approaching figure. It was Dan Joe from the Reserve. "He won't even give me a damn *nod*."

"What happened?"

"I pulled over and offered him a ride, and he wouldn't even *look* at me! Just kept walking. I'm pretty well the only person on the entire Coast who gives a *crap* about his half-baked tribe, and he can't be bothered to talk to me! I break my freakin' back for those guys—Hey!" he called to Dan Joe, who had now come within earshot. "Gimme a break. Dan, I— JESUS."

Dan Joe passed silently by. He didn't look angry, just oblivious. It was as though they didn't exist. They watched him recede, his long black braids swinging against his red flannel workshirt. The rain didn't faze him either. He kept walking.

Billy squeezed his temples as though his head were about to explode. Then he flung his woolly grey and brown Cowichan hat onto the wet pavement, where it was nearly carried off by the tug of running water. Sappho retrieved the wet thing. The raindrops were shooting down so hard now that they jumped white like sparks as they hit the pavement.

At this point Claude and Gilles wheeled by on their

soaking ten-speeds. "Ey, uh,'" hazarded Claude. "Nice pants. Where's da flood?"

Billy spun around, yelling: "Right in front of yer nose, ya moron! *Christ.* Look around ya! 'Where's the *flood*'... I ask ya."

"The fire next time," came a little voice behind them.

"What?" asked Sappho.

"Nothing," said Ruth, looking at her vinyl shoes.

Billy and Sappho drove home. There was a lot of ferry traffic. Billy sped up, angrily passing cars. Someone honked sharply, and Billy gave the driver the finger. " I'd treat a *dog* more hospitably than those Joes treat me," fumed Billy. "My friggin' *chickens* have it better." This was not saying much: Billy's chickens lived like sultans.

Billy spent the evening sitting dejectedly on the front porch of the chicken coop with a red hen resting quietly on his fluffy blond head. "Sssh, sssh," he crooned to it gently, giving Sappho a sad little wave. "Go on," he whispered. "Go on. She's asleep now." He reached his hands up and caressed the chicken with the enchanted air of someone wearing a marvelously delicate new hat. "Hush now," breathed Billy as Sappho vanished into the woods. "Hush."

In happier moods Billy played slightly irreverent games with the chickens, such as Chicken Hypnosis.

Selecting a chicken at random, Billy would set the bird down, hold its beak to the ground and draw a line in the dirt just in front of it, thereby transfixing the poor dim creature indefinitely. "The little nitwit'll sit there staring at the line 'til the cows come home if you let 'er!" But he didn't let her. After a few minutes he'd joyfully snatch up the hen and stare into its tiny glaring eyes ecstatically. "You got all the brain power of a aphid, dontcha, sweet-iepie? Bella here" (or Frances, or Lorraine, or whoever it happened to be) "is about as cunning as a flippin' rock!" Then he'd kiss the chicken and gently set it down. He instructed Finn in the chicken arts, too, and pretty soon the boy could mesmerize a red hen by drawing those lines in the dirt or put one to sleep on his small flaxen head, just like Billy had showed him. Finn would be very still lest his hat spring to life with a squawk and flap away.

Sappho peered at her face in the mirror. It peered back, hanging like a pale little moon among the branches of her long brown hair. She wielded a tube of lip-gloss. Behind her Finn appeared, looking strange. "What're you going to be for Hallowe'en?" he yelled, excited by the prospect of candy. "I'm going to be a Martian!" To his usual ensemble of overalls and a t-shirt he had added a lot of green face-paint and some silver sparkles.

"Your nose is running," she said. His nose was always running these days, perhaps because lately he spent every spare minute with the garden hose, flooding the driveway. Finn wiped at his nose with the back of his hand, smearing the makeup across his cheek.

Kate called to him from the treadle. "Finn, I think we should add a few things. Like a green cape, maybe," she called.

"No, but what're you going to be, Sappho?"

"I'm trying to get ready," she said.

"No, but WHAT?"

"Nothing. I'm too old to dress up for Hallowe'en."

"Aw*ww*!" Grumbling, Finn turned tail and clattered off again, colliding with a bureau as he went. The mirror shuddered.

They were all— the grade sixes and sevens— going on a hayride to a Hallowe'en barn dance hosted by Shelley Taylor, the most popular girl in school and a charter member of the Gang. The grade sixes and sevens were too dignified for trick-or-treating now. The town wanted to keep them off the streets on the 31st: Hallowe'en was trouble enough already without them adding to the may-hem— or so Billy had explained it, laughing hoarsely. "The least they can do is keep *you* trouble-makers off the streets on Hallowe'en. The General Store's been stocking up on eggs for weeks! Months! No-one's gettin' outta here alive!" Billy bit the pin from a phantom grenade, tossed it, then jerked around rapidly as if caught in a burst of machine-gun fire. He grabbed a broom out of the corner, returning fire and falling to the ground in a frenzy of dust and spitspray and sending a stray chair skidding across the kitchen.

"Now *cool* it, Billy," Mom had said, seeing Sappho's pupils widen into deep dark pools of fear. "You *know* she's sensitive."

Billy settled down. Panting a bit, he picked up the old hardcover book he had been carting around, *Prominent Myths of North-west Indians.* "Listen to this. This old guy, this Icelandic anthropologist, his name was Stinj Weorbun. He wrote this in 1890." Billy adjusted his little gold-rimmed spectacles. "It's great stuff. I quote: 'like virtually every people on Earth, the aboriginal tribes of the North-west coast possess a detailed conception of an under- or "other" world, a species of parallel territory which is populated by supernatural beings, among them the souls of the dead. In the case of the coastal tribes, this mirror-world may be reached through designated landmarks in this world— most commonly points in the river, but also sea-caves or other watery passages— which may be imagined as *portals* insofar as they offer a doorway onto the realm of the supernatural. These magical beings are known by a word we may translate as the Others.'"

"Hmm," murmured Kathleen fake-attentively.

"Sappho, will you do these few dishes? We need clean plates if we're going to have supper."

Billy read on: "'Of particular interest to historians is the case of a certain tribe, or people, whose version of this myth features a peculiar twist. They speak of the incursion of a whole spectral ship of Others—'"

"The rice-and-veg is nearly ready."

"No, but listen! Maybe these goddamn Joes think—"

"Look, I can't do ten things at once. I'm trying to get dinner on the— and Sappho—"

"Oh all RIGHT." That was Sappho. Billy slammed the book shut.

"It's very interesting, I just can't—"

"Forget it. *Jesus*." He began setting the table.

Back at the mirror, Sappho was going for the "windswept" look. She pinched her cheeks, bit her lips, and brushed her brown hair energetically away from her face. Tipping her head over, she brushed the underside, then flung her head back so hard that she saw stars. She looked in the mirror. Her hair was airborne, fanned out in a great wind-whipped mane. She added sweet and sticky see-through gloss to her lips, watching her hair hurrying back to its usual flat state. She was wearing a tight sky-blue t-shirt with capped sleeves, her one pair of dress pants (blue cords so high-waisted they practically covered her ribcage) and rainbow toe-socks a happy secret beneath her North Stars. Sappho added a choker of green glass beads to this outfit and tossed her hair, throwing the mirror a moody glance.

"Sapphie! Time to go!" called Kathleen. "The bus'll be down there in ten minutes!"

The path through the forest was pitch-black, dark as only a country path can be. The dark was a substance, the forest filled to the brim with it. The branches crowded in on her, whispering against her clothes. Sappho shuddered, but she knew the way by heart. It was a little lighter at the highway, with the Boley house not far off.

Intriguingly, European settlers in the region have become, in the mind of the Indian, closely identified with these uncanny "Others." Indeed, most Coast Salish dialects, the Sechelt for example, like its counterpats among the tribes other of southern British Columbia, Washington and Oregon, use the same term to describe the exotic, less than welcome newcomers.

Soon the schoolbus sailed up out of the blackness and ground to a halt, crunching over the gravel of the driveway. Sappho climbed aboard. The bus was strewn with hay: hay was scattered on and around the seats, and a couple of bales stood unwieldy in the aisle. The kids, all

Grade Sixes and Sevens, were quiet and solemn. No-one had been foolish enough to wear a Hallowe'en costume. A sober jean-blue sea lay before her, its dark depths relieved only by slippery winks of lip-gloss here and there. Sappho clambered awkwardly over a hay-bale to reach an empty seat, lurching into it headfirst as the bus pulled back onto the highway. It stopped again at Crowe Road and then near the SuperStar Mall, swallowing up kids until nearly all the Grade Sixes and Sevens were accounted for.

The Indian tends to regard his European neighbours as we might regard a sustained manifestation— unsolicited, sinister, and apparently irreversible— of elves or fairies.

Ten silent minutes later the bus was overtaken by a roaring hot rod. The driver leaned on the horn as he passed on the left. Then came another car blaring music, and Sappho peered out and saw painted faces— black, white, red, silver— hanging out the car windows. One a whiskered animal, a second with a star bursting over one eye, the third waggling and stretching his tongue from the root. Other painted faces behind them struggled to be seen.

The troubling appearance of Others on this side of the "curtain" as we may imagine it, is seen by the Indian as evidence of a serious distortion in the natural order of things.

"Kiss Army! Awright!" shouted Troy, and tugged a window down with delight, only to receive a raw egg smack in the face. Suddenly the windows of the bus were awash with eggs, smeared with yolks and pale goop and shards of white. Girls were shrieking and dropping down among the hay while the boys plastered themselves to the bleary window, delightedly yelling provocations. A white missile hurtled through the window, shattering its payload *splat* against the far wall. And then in a fresh burst of speed the car pulled ahead and vanished.

Opinion is divided among the Indians as to the cause of this imbalance, which has permitted the Others to flood across the frontier uninvited.

The girls climbed back up to their seats while the boys, ravished— their fresh cheeks hot pink with excitement, their eyes glistening— clambered down from the windows, tossing their manes into place. Sappho pulled her hair over her face like a veil and began picking bits of hay out of it.

While several tribes possess stories of troublesome Others seeking illicit entry into the Human Realm, one version in particular verges on the legendary or quasi-historical. Many tribal elders point to a notorious mis-

adventure which permits the Others, who have briefly emerged into the human world, to remain and to taint it. There is an account of what seems to be an enormous ship. The Others proffer impossibly tempting gifts, usually precious metals. Some tribe member or members accept the uncanny gifts, puncturing the coherence of their own world in so doing. This has the disastrous result of allowing the Others to gain free access to a realm not properly their own.

Only Claude and Gilles had escaped the roundup. And Michael Joe, he would never be bothered with something like a school dance. Of course pale-blue Ruth was absent ("my mom says Hallowe'en is Sat- Satan's birthday party. And anyway I'm not allowed to dance. Or eat candy." Ruth wasn't even allowed to celebrate her *own* birthday.)

How can the violated world be purified? Is some sacrifice required to atone for the misdeeds of miscreants guilty of accepting tainted, indeed accursed, gifts? Can the gifts somehow be returned? Such are the questions posed.

Strategies vary. Many of the Indians refuse to acknowledge the very existence of the European settlers, reasoning that if they find themselves ignored long enough

Sappho was not normally supposed to eat candy either. Kathleen had always met trick-or-treating with a look of apprehension which turned to sighs and eye-rolling at the first sign of candy-fuelled excitement. Billy egged her on. "The kid's on a sugar rush!" he would exclaim, laughing, and, later, when the sleepiness or moodiness set in, would add, throwing up his hands, "the kid's O.D'd on sugar." Then Kate would confiscate the candy-bag with its crackling array of offerings ranging from the sublime (mini chocolate bars) to the ridiculous (apples, peanuts, or some home-made nightmare food) and stash it, after which Sappho was allowed one treat per day. Gradually the bag was picked clean of its treasures, until all that remained were rustling wrappers and peanuts rattling neglected in their shells.

the intruders will simply

The bus pulled into Gray Star Stables, parked, and was instantly caught in a hailstorm of eggs. The driver cursed and produced a fire extinguisher. He bounded down the steps of the bus and began spraying wildly in the general direction of an old rusted tractor collapsed at some distance away. "Guy-La-Fleur!" sprang a voice from behind the tractor. "GUY! LA! FLEUR!" Sappho glimpsed two balaclava'd faces. The woolly red masks conveyed nothing, but the voices combined fear and a wild, rising joy. The figures turned tail, ran off and were quickly absorbed by the dark woods which crowded in on all sides. Their shrieking laughter echoed and finally receded.

return

Stillness reigned.

from whence they came.

The kids flicked their hair, shaking their ruffled feathers into place. Some produced fat-handled plastic combs from their back pockets, combing in smooth movements, sometimes cupping a hand behind their hair— as though listening to seashells— to get a bigger curve. They replaced their combs, they set their shoulders, they walked into the barn.

Shelley's mom had gone to a lot of trouble to decorate. The rec room was hung with sheets and strings of cotton batten which stood in for cobwebs, and the light shone blue. As a centrepiece on the table stood a grinning jack-o-lantern lit from within by a candle. A lot of store-bought food, mainly pop and chips, was fanned out gracefully on either side of the huge pumpkin. It seemed to Sappho that the horn of plenty had been emptied out there. On another table stood a record player with a small pile of 45s. Up above in the loft the hay glistered gold in its stacks and piles. Sappho heard a muffled sneeze, and then another. A small chorus of sneezes broke out.

While Sappho sidled up to the pop and chips— what wondrous armies of gaily painted bottles, what unimaginable choices— the girls moved en masse toward the record player and began examining the modest pile of singles. The boys hung back at the far side of the barn, tossing their manes like fidgety stallions and shuffling their sneakers, sneakers which were scarcely visble beneath their massive flares. Their short ski-jackets were zipped up tight, and their hands were stuffed deep in their jacket pockets.

Shelley chose a record. As the needle connected and sent the speakers crackling she moved fearlessly into the middle of the room; she was already swaying and swivelling away by the time the Bay City Rollers began chanting S-A. T-U-R. D-A-Y. *Night!* And everyone chimed in, all qualms about Les and his eyeshadow set aside. Shelley, with her tight, highwaisted flares, her blond hair feathered vertical, and her tiny black t-shirt with the slogan "A Touch of Class" scripted across her chest, a single red rose stretched out below— this girl seemed to

Sappho to be laquered with power. She possessed all the smoothly molded shapeliness, all the glow, all the bright impermeability of a toystore creation. The fact that her sharp-shell teeth jostled slightly for space only rendered her all the more perfect somehow. Shelley's gold-velour flesh was pulled tightly across the rise of her facial bones, and her brown eyes were fixed on some far horizon as she danced there impervious to shame, and soon, soon enough the rest of the girls trickled onto the floor. The boys followed soon after.

Bobbing well above the crowd was Troy. His face was washed, his cool restored. He was looking suddenly and inexplicably tall and swaying like a stilt-walker. Sappho looked at his feet. The curtains of his pant-legs parted briefly to reveal an impressive pair of tobacco-brown plat-form boots, whether ankle-length or knee-length Sappho could not tell. Troy, who had been Shelley's boyfriend for almost an entire month, swayed up and stood with her at the centre of the undulating and chorusing group; when the embarrassing pause between songs arrived he flipped his shiny light brown hair back so violently that he stumbled and put a heel through his pant-leg. There was a tearing sound and then some static from the re-cord player. And then, as Troy shook his foot to free his pant-leg and Shelley continued to stare ahead as if noticing nothing, "Saturday Night" by the Bay City Rollers came on again. And again. And again. It was the only song they played—not that anyone regretted it. The only interruption was Shelley's announcement that Troy had given her a Mood Ring for Hallowe'en. She held up her left hand to confirm it:. Troy and Shelley were absolutely and irrefutably Going Around.

That was the night Shelley first took notice of Sappho. Because of the Ouija board. After they had all been dancing for two hours, and their throats were sore and their voices hoarse from shouting Bay City Rollers lyrics over and over again, and a few couples like Shelley and Troy were beginning to lean into corners, and kids were beginning to be beckoned away by parents who came in their station-wagons and trucks, Mrs. Taylor appeared and turned down the volume. Then she turned up the lights and motioned her daughter over to the centre of the room. Mrs. Taylor looked nice, thought Sappho. She pictured her own mom wearing that orange cowl-neck sweater and brown cord maxi-skirt with high-heeled boots. But Kate didn't like store-bought clothes.

"Shelley has an invitation for the rest of the *girls*, don't you honey?"

"Already?" Shelley kicked a little at the ground.

"Yes, *already*. It's past ten o'clock!" said her mother in a stage whisper. "Now go ahead!"

"Um, okay. You girls can come over and see our rec room if you want."

Sappho had never seen anything like the Taylor family rec room. It was sumptuously outfitted with wall-to-wall cream shag carpet. There were two beanbag chairs, a leather couch and some enormous pillows on the floor. It was as though Shelley had been a teenager for years, as though she were sixteen instead of barely twelve. There were black-light posters on the fake wood-panelled walls, and a big cork board with all kinds of photos and Sports Day ribbons— blue, all blue— pinned to it in a neat array. Shelley had the run of the rec-room. In honour of the guests there stood another table groaning with board games and pop and chips and candy. Mrs. Taylor told them to dig in, and Sappho chose a candy necklace. The room, the house itself, with all its perfectly machined shapes and gloss and everything smelling of plastic and sugar and artificial flavours, was deliciously alien to Sappho. With the air of one exploring a new planet she slowly crept around the room.

Finally Sappho sat on the couch and selected an issue of *Creem* magazine from a stack. The cover showed Kiss posing like superheroes, heads held high and defiant and legs planted wide. She thumbed through the magazine and chewed on her candy necklace.

"Those are Dana's," said Lisa, frowning.

"Oh— sorry—"

"Dana is her brother. He died in a car accident," continued Lisa reproachfully. "He drowned. His body was missing for days." She pointed to a school portrait pinned to the corkboard. "That's Dana," she added, her tone reverent. He really loved Kiss."

Sappho set the magazine back in its pile and went to look at the photo, with its sky-like blue backdrop, which showed a very good-looking boy wearing a Kiss t-shirt. The lost boy had blond feathered hair, deep-set brown eyes and a sharp rise to his cheekbones. He was smiling, just enough to reveal his dimples, Shelley's dimples. His lips were turned up and slightly parted, as though he were about to speak.

Shelley joined them in front of the photo. "I've been trying to talk to him," she said to no-one in particular. "I know there's something he wants to tell me."

"How— how have you—"

Shelley smiled knowingly at Lisa. Lisa smiled back and, still holding Shelley's gaze, said "With the Ouija board."

"But so far it hasn't worked," she added. Their faces went blank. "One time I think the thing kind of moved a little."

Sappho ventured a suggestion. "Well but maybe *tonight*...."

Shelley and Lisa locked eyes again. Tonight was Hallowe'en.

Maybe tonight.

Lisa fetched a box from the closet. It contained the Ouija board, with its alphabet painted in a wide arch over the top, its numbers ranged along the bottom. The board came with funny object about the size of a child's hand. It was roughly heart-shaped and had three short felt-tipped legs, so it sat like a doll's coffee table. "It's called the pointer," said Lisa. "You place your fingertips on it, like this"— she demonstrated— and it's supposed to move around and point at the letters." The Ouija board was sitting on a footstool; Shelley and Lisa were cross-legged on the floor.

"Okay. Now everyone hush up and concentrate," said Shelley. All the girls sat obediently down on the snowy shag carpet and squeezed their eyes shut.

Shelley said quietly, "Is anyone here with us?"

Silence. The pointer was still.

"Hello? Is anyone listening?"

Nothing. Shelley sighed. Lisa let go. "It doesn't work," she said. "It's so *fake*."

Sappho reached out: "Can I try?"

Shelley shrugged.

Sappho touched the pointer and asked "Are you there?"

Everyone squealed as the pointer shot across the room.

"You threw it!" cried Lisa.

"I did *not*." Sappho retrieved the pointer from a bowl of chips and wiped it clean with a paper napkin.

Shelley had flushed pink. "Shut up, *Lisa*. She never threw it. Bring it back, Sappho."

A few of the girls crept upstairs, silent on the muffling carpet.

Sappho set up the board again and Shelley asked, "Who are you?"

Slowly but decisively, the pointer began to spell.

Dana Taylor was sixteen when the car crash took him. Sixteen and sweet, though like lots of other teenagers on the Coast he liked to tear up the highway in his hot rod. And rip along old and treacherous logging routes that scarred the mountainside every which way, roads where nobody went anymore except the teenagers to their bush parties. Dana and his buddy Gord liked to roar down the highway at 100 miles an hour, spin tight circles in the gravel outside the RCMP detachment and speed off, disappearing up some old road before the cops even managed to set down their coffee cups. The boys loved that— rattling cages. One night, while Dana drove, Gordie hung out the back seat window and poured a little trail of gas right down the centre of the highway, from the ferry dock clear to the SuperStar, almost. Then struck a match and dropped it. And they shivered with joy as the whole snaking highway shot into flames, becoming a whole snaking yellow wall of fire. It nearly took the bridge out, that blaze. The Volunteer Fire Department were up all night.

Dana's body knew every bend and slant of that highway, when he would lean and when he would lurch. Each time he drove the highway, the turns pressed him caressingly this way and that— against the seat, against the door. Until it took him. One familiar lurch near the bridge suddenly wasn't, and became a long drawn arc through space. The car tore through railings—leaving them hanging like the stiff claws of branches— and into the river. Just where the sweet water mixes with the salt.

Why did he drown? He could swim; his family knew that. Was it the spirits? Potato spirit, sugar spirit, even cactus spirit—Dana 's body was drenched from within, drenched from without. So once they had finally, finally retrieved his corpse from the water and laid it in the earth, that's what the Taylor family told themselves: it was the spirits. It was the spirits.

"A— S—K. Ask. M— E—. Me. Ask me."

"Ask me what?"

"I bet we're supposed to ask it questions, like who's there and stuff."

Shelley was talking, and Lisa was talking, but Sappho was saying nothing. She barely breathed as the pointer slid from letter to letter, her fingers hardly touching it. She had to reach to keep up with it.

"Who are you?" hazarded Shelley.

The pointer trembled and gave a little swirl, like a dancer tracing a toe on the floor.

"Are you— is it— is it you? Is it you?"

The pointer shot to NO. And then it spelled some more.

"I-T-S-N-O-T-M-E," read Lisa from behind them. "It's not me. What's that supposed to mean?"

"It's confused," said Sappho.

"Whaddya mean, 'it'? Dana was a *guy*," Lisa shot back. *You're* the 'it', *Lesbo!*"

Shelley kicked Lisa in the shin. "What is *wrong* with you, you titless bitch?"

There were more little screams as the pointer shot off the board and landed with a splash in a bowl of Kool-Aid. Shelley ran upstairs to find her mom. Lisa just stared at Sappho poisonously.

After a few minutes Sappho unglued herself from her chair and fished out the pointer, sticky with flavour crystals. The little felt pads were of course soaked through.

"We'll have to wait for it to dry," she observed.

"We'll use a blow-dryer," said Lisa. "DUH."

Mrs. Taylor came hurrying in with a dishtowel in one

hand and a smoke in the other. "Mom, " said Shelley, "Lisa's acting like a bitch."

Mrs. Taylor's sigh was raw with smoking. "Language, Shelley. Well girls, it's been great having you, but your parents'll be wanting to pick you up." Several of the girls trooped off to make phone-calls.

Mrs. Taylor's voice dropped down low as she turned to Lisa. "Go on next-door now. We'll talk about this later." Lisa started lacing up her Pepsi shoes. "And girls, quit playin' with that friggin' board. You know I hate it. Gives me the creeps."

" Sorry, Mom," said Shelley winningly. "It is Hallowe'en! Mom, please may Sappho stay overnight?"

"Sure thing, we just have to give her folks a call. What's your number, honey?"

"We don't have a phone," said Sappho.

Everyone looked at her.

"You mean it's broken?" offered Mrs. Taylor.

"We— my— Billy doesn't believe in.... we just don't have a phone," Sappho finished weakly. How could she explain the whole Back to the Land thing?

"Well, what a darn shame. We'll just have to drive down and see ol' Billy Black, won't we?

Mrs. Taylor drove Sappho home in the family station wagon, which was decorated, a bit like the rec room, with fake wood panelling. Mrs. Taylor plied her cigarette and looked thoughtful. She was thin and pretty with streaked hair and a fine tracery of lines around her brown eyes. It was just the two of them. Mrs. Taylor said, "You know, ever since Russ made foreman at the mill, life's been pretty comfy for the Taylor family. We've got a lovely home and even a stake in Gray Star Stables, so I can spend every spare minute with horses, just like I dreamed it when I was a kid—" she laughed her smoky laugh—"but back when he was a lumberjack money was real tight, and every day, I prayed like anything they wouldn't bring my darling man home in pieces."

Sappho pictured this sadly. Then she remembered how Dana died, how they must have brought him home, bloated and waterlogged. Tears sprang to her eyes.

Mrs. Taylor was still talking. "And hey, my daddy was a lumberjack back in the days when lumberjacks didn't pull much money in. Yeah, we were pretty damn poor when *I* was a kid, too."

"Oh," Sappho said softly, imagining Mrs. Taylor wearing shoe-boxes on her frosty feet, Mrs. Taylor without a bed to call her own.

"I remember our phone got cut off practically every month," Mrs. Taylor continued, laughing just a little. "The heat too!"

"Oh. Oh. It's not exactly like that, Mrs. Taylor—"

Sappho didn't think they were poor, although in

a way they were. But that wasn't why they had no phone. "It's just that Billy— it's like in *Little House on the Prairie*. He made our house. He makes everything. But he's a student —"

"Pretty darn long in the tooth to be a student, though, eh?" She laughed huskily, sidling her mascara'd eyes over to let Sappho in on the joke, nudging her. "Anyway, no offense, okay hon? No offense. And call me Barb."

They drove on through the deep night in easy silence.

"It's nothing to be ashamed of," resumed Barb after a few miles."None of it, no-how. Where is that driveway? I wish that asshole would turn his high beams off." A car bearing down in the opposite lane flooded them in light as they approached the bridge, and they sat frozen like rabbits until the dark came down again. "Pardon my French." She turned to Sappho and laughed again. Sappho laughed back.

The station-wagon turned into the steep driveway to Chickenland and plowed on through the forest, running the gauntlet of trees and bushes and ferns which dragged at its sides ("Someone should get in here with a backhoe, hon!") and finally emerged into the clearing where the coops and cabins lay haphazardly, so very haphazardly. Thus it now seemed to Sappho as she saw their place with altered eyes, and she flushed hot to see it like that, such a jumble, every detail raggedy and unfinished.

Every rail, frame and shingle eked out by hand, every detail splayed at odd angles to every other one. Nothing here boasted the machined sleekness of the Taylor stuff.

Billy appeared silhouetted in the doorway. He beckoned Barb into the house.

Sappho couldn't hear much. Billy was talking rapidly in a low voice. Barb was nodding slowly. She looked pensive. Then they turned to Sappho, who got out of the car, walked over and wrapped her arms around Billy's waist.

"Your mom is back at Gray Star General for observation, Sappho," he half-whispered. "Don't worry. She's gonna be okay, but the doctor wants her there. It's best for the baby to have all nine months! She's gotta keep perfectly still."

"Your mom is a strong lady," offered Barb.

As Barb was leaving, she hugged Sappho and kissed her cheek. Sappho could smell a nice store-bought perfume. "You are always welcome at our home," Barb said. "You can have a sleepover real soon."

Pulling away from the A-frame, she braked and called "Bye now." Then she stepped on the gas, and the dark forest swiftly gulped the station wagon back into itself.

Sappho would stay close to Billy as they waited for Kathleen to stop, in the white sheets, under the greenish lights, to stop cramping.

"Goodnight, Billy," she called down from the loft, pulling the blankets up to her chin. "I love you."

"Love *you*, little gal," he replied. "And so do all these damn chickens."

Chapter Six

A few nights later, instead of watching the Boley kid tumble as if magnetized to the river, she watched Dana's passage. She saw him come to the other world from her waiting-place among rocks deep beneath the water. She saw the Mustang as a shadow above before it sliced into the deeps. The car sank slowly, and she shimmied up to meet him. Huge air bubbles escaped from within the car, taking Dana's last chances with them. Unless he grew gills like hers. She reached the windshield, waving her whitened limbs to the boy she knew to be there, though it was dark within and hard to see anything. Suddenly, there were his hands, pushing against the glass as though it would soon break and release him. It was getting harder and harder to see: long swathes of inky hair floated before her eyes. It was getting harder to hear: her ears were filled with insistent music.

Drowning/

She kicked upwards
in a sea of love/
to break the surface
to heave herself onto the riverbank and find herself flopping wet and gasping in her own bed.

Downstairs, a woman was singing.

"Mom?" spluttered Sappho, full of shaky hope.

The woman sang on. "*... where everyone/ would love to drown/...*"

Sappho wriggled wet-eyed and sweating to the edge of the loft and looked over. There, warming herself in a sunbeam that illuminated her cape of hair, lounged Nancy on Kate and Billy's bed. She was combing the long pale stuff. A red hen sat on the pudgy armchair, pecking idly at this and that.Now, weirdly, Nancy was pulling individual hairs from the comb and placing them carefully on the bed. Sappho felt chilly. She peered over at Finn's cot. His eyes were wide and he lay frozen. Sappho caught his stare and held it. They hadn't seen Nancy since the big brawl at the Goon Saloon. The last time they had seen her, she was cursing in the back of an RCMP cruiser. Sappho looked at Finn and rested one cheek on her hands, closing her eyes. Obediently, he feigned sleep. Sappho crawled back to the edge and peeked down.

Nancy was rearranging the bedclothes. Then she produced a small vial and shook it over them. Her favourite scent, a pungent Indian oil, thickened the air. When she was finished with the bed, it didn't seem very neat. Then she turned her attention to the dresser, moving things around a bit. Was she looking for something?

Sappho heard Billy's truck pull into the clearing, and she crawled to the window. She watched him get out and go around to the passenger side, open the door, and lift out Kathleen. He carried her towards the front door. Sappho wanted to clamber down, but she was afraid.

Nancy, still humming, seemed unfazed. She crossed the room and opened the door. Billy lumbered through.

"What the hell are you doing in my place, *Nancy*?"

"Gosh, Billy," she replied in her most girlish voice. "What a funny question!"

"You're up to something, dammit! And will you quit letting the chickens into the cabin? They're spoiled enough as it is!" Billy was still holding Kate in his arms.

Kate sighed loudly. "Look, I just don't have the energy for this..."

"Sorry, Katie. Let's get you into bed."

"Yes, Billy! What is *wrong* with you? Put your lady-love to bed!" Nancy left, slamming the door. Six or seven chickens remained.++

For a few minutes, neither of them spoke. Billy had no bluster left in him, it seemed. Kate sighed again.

"Billy..."

And again: "Billy... trying to take the baby to term is hard enough... without that woman... hanging around."

"*I* didn't invite her here! Hon, I *know* how hard this is—"

Kate's voice went sharp. "No. No, you do NOT know how hard this is! You don't know how hard it is to keep a baby growing inside you, that's for damn sure, and you DON'T know what it is like to have her hanging around insinuating things all the time! Oh, what kind of mess have I fallen into here?"

"Look, I warned you to watch out for her. She's dangerous. She doesn't want you to have the baby—isn't that obvious? I bet my eyeteeth that tea she gave was you pennyroyal. Or is that so hard to believe of a 'sister'? Lemme tell ya, she is NOT your sister!"

"Okay, Billy. Okay." Kate sounded frosty. "I believe it. But answer me this: WHY? She's screwed every guy in Gray Star. Why is she so hell-bent on getting rid of *me*? What is BETWEEN you two—apart from the obvious, I mean?"

Billy did not answer for a minute. "Geez... it's a long story. Nancy's a... she's a Yank like me, and we just..."

"Just what? Just what? What was going on here before I came? Is Finn—"

Billy's voice dropped to a whisper: "*Katie, let's not put the kids through this. They're right upstairs. You 'n me, we'll clear this thing up, I promise. Okay?*"

And Kate, looking up to the loft and seeing two anxious faces appear, agreed. And there was peace for a few minutes.

But then she found the first strawberry blond hair. And the second. There was hair draped all over the double bed. She sniffed the air. It was thick with Nancy's perfumed Indian oil. Sliding between the sheets, she gave a start and yanked the blankets aside. Nancy's turquoise necklace was coiled there on the mattress. Billy sat heavily down on the couch and covered his face with his hands.

Kate moved to the armchair. "I can't get in this bed. It's not mine now," she whispered.

"We'll wash everything. *I'll* wash everything." Doing laundry was an all-day affair at Chickenland, and Kate, feeble now, wouldn't be strong enough for any of it: chopping wood, firing the woodstove, heating the water on it in a huge pan... the drying might take two days in the autumn weather.

"Billy."

"Yeah."

"Drop me off at the StarSpray Motel, will you?"

"Aw, Kate... "

"I just need to rest... my mind. The doctor told me to relax. I can't afford... this."

So Billy picked her up again and walked to the door. As they left, two chickens muscled their way in. For once

Billy did not take any notice of his chickens, just nudged the door shut with his foot. Sappho and Finn heard the pickup roar to life and then recede down the hill. The ferry traffic got loud for a while.

They spent the afternoon hypnotizing chickens.

At sundown Billy returned. Behind him drove Mrs. Taylor—Barb— who waved at the kids, and leaned against her car, smoking and waiting in the light of the magic hour—that time near sundown when the light is both peachy and lilac.

Billy sat Sappho down on the couch for a moment. He crouched and hugged her. Sappho saw with misery that he had been crying, and that he was trying not to cry now. His voice was cracking with effort. "Sapph darlin', your mom is safe and sound at the StarSpray Motel. It's as clean as any hospital room there, and I've got the manager lady lookin' in on her. But I think she wants to stay there for a while—the baby is due real soon, ya know."

"Oh Billy, I should have said—I should have said when you were fighting—"

"It's nothin' to do with you—"

"But we saw Nancy in the house. She was combing her hair out and saving the strands. She was doing something to the bed—"

"Look, Sapph. Listen to me. I know she messed with our place. I haven't touched that woman—well, since I met your mother, I haven't looked at another woman. Actually, I bet your mom knows that. But lemme tell ya, she's tired. Kate's better off at the motel for a bit," his voice was cracking badly, "even if—even if—"

"Why is Nancy even here? I thought she was in jail!"

"Yeah, well… it ain't so easy to keep people in jail. Turns out the Mounties are havin' a helluva time getting' ol' Cowboy Cal to say a word against her. Maybe he loves her, maybe he's afraid of her, or maybe he just plain just doesn't want the hair-plug disaster story written up in *The Beachcomber* and trumpeted up and down the coast some more. But the social workers are still on Nancy's case for neglecting our boy Finn, so there's a bright spot." Billy choked out a laugh. "Anyway, Sapphie, how 'bout you go and spend a few nights at the Taylors—just until things settle down. Me 'n Finn will camp out together. And you can go to school and get three squares a day."

Sappho collapsed sideways on the couch. She clung to Billy, tears spilling into her ears, down her cheeks and into the corners of her mouth. She tasted salt. She cried for her mother, so fragile, and Billy, so crumpled. She didn't mind going with Mrs. Taylor. She liked Mrs. Taylor—Barb. But she cried just the same. What would happen to them all?

Eventually Billy, his arm around her shoulders, guided her down the trail to Barb's car. Barb hugged her, cradling Sappho's brown head in her sweet, clean-smelling neck. Then the two of them drove back to the Taylor house in silence. Whenever it was safe, when the curves smoothed out for a moment, Barb reached over the gearshift and squeezed Sappho's hand. They turned down the driveway and the big new Taylor ranch house hoved into view. Sappho helped unpack the station wagon, which was full of grocery bags from the SuperStar. Together they put the groceries away—eight bags' worth. Barb put her in a bedroom Sappho knew to be Dana's. There were no mementoes in the room, no collage of snapshots or brass-dipped baby boots; no school pennants or trophies lovingly dusted. But she knew it was Dana's room all the same.

Just as Sappho was getting dozy, Shelley looked in on her. She sat on the edge of the bed, fresh from the shower, resplendent in pink pajamas and bunny slippers. Shelley reached over and touched Sappho's long straight hair. "You know," she said thoughtfully, "your hair could feather quite nicely." And then: "We should go to the mall this weekend. The new hairdresser is a guy from Town.

"C'mon to my room for a sec. I'm gonna blowdry my hair." Sappho rolled out of Dana's bed and followed Dana's sister to her deluxe chamber. Shelley had a big, canopied bed piled high with throw pillows and stuffed animals. There was a wide vanity bureau and ruffled curtains. All the fabric—curtains, linens, bedskirt—was pink.

"Oh," breathed Sappho. "It's so pretty."

"Thanks. My mom sewed most of this stuff. She always made our curtains and everything. Dana had hockey players on his. My room was lavender before... anyway, this year Mom worked like crazy to make it over. She likes to keep busy."

"My mom sews really nice costumes."

"For, like, Hallowe'en?" said Shelley, reaching for her blowdryer and plugging it in beside the vanity. "When you were a little kid?"

"Um, yeah..."

"Neat." Shelley pointed at a glossy poster of Charlie's Angels pinned near the mirror. "I copy Farrah. When we get your hair feathered, you can copy Jaclyn."

"Wow, thanks!" Sappho, who thought Jaclyn Smith was the most beautiful woman in the world, was hugely flattered.

"Hey, you've even got the same last name as her! That's gotta mean something for sure."

Sappho glowed with pleasure.

"I told Lisa she could be Jaclyn. But I guess she'll have to be the other one now," Shelley giggled carelessly. This was a low blow. Nobody wanted to be the other one. The two girls shared a glance of complicity through the mirror. Then Shelley got down to business, shrieking dryer in one hand, round brush in the other. The feathering was an intense operation: each piece, starting with the shortest ones at the top, had to be rolled around the brush and dried separately. Then for a full minute Shelley turned the dryer full on her face and shut her eyes, and Sappho watched the girl's reflection, rapt, as the blond hair fanned and flowed and streamed behind her.

"I pretend like I'm on the back of a Harley," said Shelley, shutting off the dryer and opening her eyes. "In California. Or Hawaii maybe." She flopped onto the bed, using a plush pony to cushion her golden head.

"Is Troy driving?"

"I dunno... is there ice hockey in Hawaii?" Shelley flopped on her populous bed and selected a stuffed bear to hold. "It could be Leif Garrett. He's the cutest boy ever. Hey—ask the Magic Eight-Ball if I'll get to meet Leif!" she said, giggling, and nodded her head towards the black device, which sat among the hairspray canisters and makeup. "It'll totally work for *you*, Sappho."

"Okay." Sappho picked up the Magic Eight-Ball, turned it upside down, and asked aloud: "Will Shelley meet Leif Garrett?" She righted it and watched the message float into view. NO, it read.

"Well? What does it say?"

"It says YES."

"Way to go, Sappho! We better start planning the wedding right away."

Sappho shook the Magic Eight-ball before replacing it.

Shelley yawned, covering her mouth politely.

"Well, I'd better go to bed. Goodnight," said Sappho, turning to the door.

But Shelley was already asleep. Sappho switched off the lamp with the big ruffled pink shade Barb had made so lovingly, leaving her new friend asleep in the soft rays of the night-light. She closed the door and returned to Dana's room.

Instead of going to the Unisex Salon at the mall that weekend, Shelley and Sappho went horseback riding. "Zorro needs exercise, Shelley Taylor," said her mother, as the three of them ate Fruit Loops around the immaculate orange Formica kitchen table. "Remember our deal."

Shelley rolled her eyes.

"I saw that, young lady. Don't you go all spoiled on me. Lord, what I did to get on horseback when I was your age! Worked mucking out stalls for rich folks for nothing—- or as near as, just so I could have the privilege of exercising the horses."

With the jaded air of one who had heard this story

many times, Shelley sighed loudly and rolled her eyes again. "Then why don't *you* take him out today?"

"Because, as you perfectly well know, I have a whole *mess* of things to attend to down at the stables. And when you begged me for your own horse you also agreed to care for him—at least on weekends. So get your darn riding things on and find some gear for our guest. Chop-chop." Barb began loading the dishwasher.

It was a rare sunny autumn day—"perfect for a trail-ride", as Barb said, driving the short stretch of highway that separated the Taylor home from the stables. "You're gonna love it, hon," she said, turning swiftly back to flash a grin at Sappho. "I wish to heck I could be with you. But we've got the farrier here today and a whole bunch of horses to shoe." Sappho, who had been drawing horses for years—horses with elaborately wavy manes and tails aflutter, horses with wings, horses with garlands, horses with princesses atop their jeweled saddles—but had no experience beyond the pony rides at Stanley Park, felt thrilled but nervous. She was wearing an old pair of boot-cut bluejeans, cowboy boots, two sweaters, a jean-jacket and a red bandanna— all supplied by Shelley, whose own riding clothes were mostly white. Sappho thought idly of the big new washer and dryer set vibrating away at all hours just off the Taylor family rec room. As the station wagon passed under a wooden horseshoe-encrusted arch (folksy letters spelt Gray Star Stables) and pulled into the yard, Sappho spied a huge black horse galloping around the corral. "There's our pride and joy," said Barb. "He's a bit frisky for a beginner, though. Shelley, you ride Zorro and put our guest on Teddy."

Teddy turned out to be a compact horse, light brown with black mane and tail. A Buckskin, Sappho learned. "We'll ride western," said Shelley, and disappeared into the barn, returning shortly with intricately embossed saddles and harnesses, "but first we groom. This is the boring part. C'mon." Taking a bucket of brushes and assorted instruments, Shelley showed Sappho what to do, talking all the while. Sappho liked brushing Teddy, and she worked on him until he gleamed, pausing to wrap her arms around his wide neck. He smelled good. She watched Shelley pick his hooves clean while she gave him a sugarcube from her flattened palm as she'd been taught.

"Don't worry, he's a vegetarian," puffed Shelley, bent over Teddy's upturned hoof. "If he bites your fingers, it's definitely a mistake." She tacked up both horses and supplied Sappho with a white cowboy hat to match her own. Seated on Teddy, who no longer seemed to be on the short side, Sappho was glad for the saddle-horn. They set off. She gripped the horn with one hand and tried to ply the reins with the other.

"The thing you have to know about horses," called Shelley, turning around, "is that they're always expecting a cougar to jump on their back. They can spook at some tiny thing, like a plastic bag flapping on the ground or whatever. They can bolt, or just jump sideways and knock you into the bushes! Just be calm and show him you're in charge."

Teddy stopped abruptly and bent his head to graze.

"Pull him up! He's testing you." Sappho pulled up on the reins, but Teddy kept eating. Sappho tugged; Teddy munched. Finally, obeying a command from Shelley, he started walking again.

Shelley and Zorro led the way through the woods, along a trail which ran roughly parallel to the river. The trail inclined upwards—they were headed for the powerline, the realm of civet-cats and cougars and bears. And Sasquatches. Sappho stroked Teddy's neck, murmuring that everything would be fine, nothing would eat him—not while Shelley was there.

After a while, she relaxed enough to look around her. The trees were getting bigger, towering cedars and dark green spruce smelling like Christmas. A lot of alder grew along the path. Sometimes she had to duck to avoid being swiped by overhanging branches. They passed huge logs thick with deep furry moss, little ferns and fungus. They passed swampy areas studded with gaseous yellow skunk cabbage. The sword ferns grew massive here. Sappho could imagine dinosaurs stomping through this landscape.

"Here we are," said Shelley after a while. They rode into a sunny clearing. Around the clearing stood weather-beaten shacks—abandoned homesteads, Shelley explained. "This is my secret place. Even Lisa's never seen it. So don't tell her about it, okay?"

"Okay," replied Sappho, flattered. They hitched up the horses and explored the shacks. People had gone to some trouble here, fostering garden plants like rhododendrons and strawberries and rosebushes. There were fruit-trees too—apple and plum and pear, Shelley said. All those were running wild now. The rainforest was absorbing them into its mix, just as it was rapidly reclaiming the homesteads, sending moss and vines up the walls and seedlings everywhere. The roofs, blanketed with years of fallen leaves, were sinking, and some had collapsed.

"Who lived here?" asked Sappho, captivated.

"Pioneers, I guess. But why were they so far from the sea? Sometimes I think they were outlaws." Inside one shack they found clippings stuck to the walls—pretty girls from old magazine ads, mostly. They also found pots and pans and mildewed furniture. It was as if the homesteaders had pulled up stakes suddenly, leaving much of what they owned. And at every opening—windows, cracks in the walls and in the floor, plants were pushing through.

"It's a ghost-town," said Sappho.

Barb had packed lunches. Shelley took them from the saddlebags, and they ate at the centre of the clearing—peanut butter and jam sandwiches on soft white bread, fruit cocktail in little plastic cups, a can of Coke each.

They put the garbage back in the saddlebags, and left the secret place as they had found it. "Promise not to tell anyone," said Shelley, and Sappho crossed her heart, glad to have a secret to keep.

If she had designed a perfect day with a perfect friend, it could not have been better than that. After the untacking, the drive home, the shower which rinsed away the deeply grassy smell of horses and a lot of horsehair, Sappho sat at Dana's desk and went to work drawing a felt-pen picture that would do justice to the day. She drew her flying horse with all the colours she could manage. Upon his back was a proudly seated super-girl with a flowing cape, her yellow hair feathered at precisely the same angle to the magic animal's feathered wings. Hands were hard to do, but luckily she could hide them in the waving mane—the rider was gripping it. The horse, front hoof bent, was about to alight on a mountaintop. She was working on the boots—not riding boots at all really, more like knee-high platforms—when Shelley opened the door. Lisa was behind her. Sappho covered the drawing with a book.

In spite of Mrs. Taylor's dislike of the Ouija board, Shelley and Lisa had lost no time in producing it again.

"You guys," said Sappho hesitantly, "maybe we shouldn't. I think it could be weird. Like, dangerous."

Shelley looked thoughtful.

"Oh, I *knew* she'd jam out!" Lisa sneered.

"No, it's just, like, Shelley's mom thinks it's creepy."

"Well, DUH. It's a Ouija board, you idiot. Anyway, who are you to tell Shelley what her mom likes or hates? Who do you think you are? You're barely even in Grade Seven!"

Shelley frowned. "Don't talk like that to our guest, okay, Lisa? How would you like it if I came over and yelled at your houseguests? Now shut up and let me think." She was quiet for a moment.

"You know, my mom doesn't know *why* we want to talk to the Ouija board," she said. "And we shouldn't tell her, not yet anyway. But I think maybe she would understand if she knew we were trying to find out what really happened to my brother," she went on meditatively. "I mean, my mom and dad are always asking questions. Like, how come he drowned if he could swim so well? Dana was training to be a lifeguard. His Speedos were covered with Participaction patches. He had bronze, silver and gold before he was twelve. How come he drowned? And his body vanished for three days. How did his body get so far out to sea, even with the undertow?"

Lisa's scorn turned to wheedling. "Yeah, Sappho. The Taylors have a right to find out the true story."

"I guess. But why—"

"—do you have to play?"Lisa took a step towards her. "Because it only works when you're here, that's why!"

They went into the rec room. It was windy outside. In the faintest of light Sappho could see the treetops tossing. The darkness was coming down, hanging in the cedars like smoke. The trees raked their fingers against the sliding-glass doors. Sappho saw the whole scene reflected in that glass panorama: herself, Shelley and Lisa cross-legged, their rainbow toe-socks vivid against the wall-to-wall white shag, the Ouija with its pointer on the glass coffee-table, where it jostled for space with Coke bottles and a bowl of salt-n-vinegar potato chips; Kiss posters on the walls. Outside was invisible now. Before the reflection revealed any more presences, she closed her eyes and put her left hand on the pointer.

"Dana, is there anything you need to tell us?" she whispered.

Lisa snorted. "It's more like what *we* need to know from *him*—"

"No, I can feel he wants to tell us something," cut in Shelley, her voice low. She placed her right hand gently on the pointer.

The pointer began to slide across the board. Lisa stuffed back her shrieks with a white leather pillow.

"S-T-U-C-K," read Shelley, as the pointer made its looping progress. "Oh geez, what does that mean? Like he's caught and he can't breathe? Like he's drowning?" She sounded pretty short of breath herself.

"It's just one word. It could mean lots of stuff. Don't worry," said Sappho, concentrating. The river, always the river. "Tell us about the water," she murmured. The pointer was moving again, fast now. But it wasn't Dana talking.

The Salmon Princess was sixteen when the Others broke through—suddenly, in a boat bigger than anyone had ever seen or told of. One morning she awoke and walked the path to the river, as she did every morning, and there it was, floating where the river met the ocean. She stood among the trees and watched. The Others seemed to be in the act of swimming up from below, swimming up from their passageway through the river-bed, for most of them were in the river, diving and playing in the water. The current pushed hard toward the sea, but the Others were strong. Some of the males—they were all males, these Others; there were no females—were naked and scrubbing their phantom-white skins with sand

and rocks. And the Others must have been thirsty for human water, for some were crouching all along the riverbed and gulping furiously.

The Salmon Princess had met the Others in frightening dreams: here they were. They were a pale underground tribe, blanched from living in the darkness, through now their white skin had already darkened in places, even after only a few minutes under the hot eye of the sun. Some of them had hair like fire, like dancing flames—were they burning in the heat and light, their fire-hair standing on end? If they were burning, they did not seem to feel pain. They were laughing and calling to each other in their Other language, not shrieking and hopping around in horror as she had once seem a fellow Salmon Person do when the fire leapt up his robe one black night. The manifestation of the Others— it was all utterly terrifying, she could admit that to herself, although she was a Princess and too proud to show fear outwardly.

Everyone knew that the Others yearned to cross over, and that in the distant past they had managed to put their toes across the threshold more than once, but the shape of things stayed solid; the frontiers held fast. No longer. What had gone wrong? Why were they here? How had they passed from their river caves into the human realm so quickly and completely? She had hoped never to see the Others in her lifetime, breathing the air she breathed and treading the earth she trod. She had hoped, but all the while she had known that sooner or later they would come.

Running would not solve anything. There was a tear in the weave of creation, and all she could do now was approach, face the Others and somehow persuade them to go back to the riverbed, travel through the caves and pass over the borders, go back to their underground by-ways. A Salmon Princess could do no less.

She stepped out of the woods and into the open.

One of the Others, stepping onto the bank while the rest remained in the river, turned and gazed at her. His eyes were startling, blue-gray as the water that had churned him up into the human realm. After gazing at her for a while in silence, he reached into the folds of his clothing and pulled something out. He opened his hand to reveal some things she could not name. He extended the hand further. The strange objects gleamed in the sun, shiny as the flanks of a young salmon. They looked like huge scales, the impenetrable scales of a deathless fish. Did this Other one know she was the Salmon Princess? The Other was smiling and wagging his head. Clearly, he knew. Slowly she drew her hands out of her robe and cupped them together.

"T-A-K-E-B-A-C-K-T-H-E-S-I-L-V-E-R. Take back the silver. T-A-K-E-B-A-C-K-T-H-E-S-I-L-V-E-R. Take back the silver. W-E-" But as Sappho spoke the words aloud, the pointer shot off the coffee table and hit the sliding glass doors with a bang. At that instant, someone tapped the glass from the outside. The girls screamed.

Their screams were answered with falsetto howls and laughter. Sappho's scalp and nape were tight with goosebumps.

"It's the stupid *boys!*" cried Shelley, crossing the room. "Quit laughing, Troy! It's not funny!"

The sliding glass door opened a crack and Troy pushed his way through. Shelley made a half-hearted effort to block them, but Claude and Gilles popped through immediately. They were bursting with energy. After a pause, Michael Joe slid through, the picture of indifference. The trespassers smelled of woodsmoke, cigarettes, sea-salt; at the same time, they smelled distinctly sugary. Sappho knew the sugar-spirit smell from the Goon Saloon. She felt a tide of nausea and excitement creep high within her. Troy, Claude and Gilles were doubled over with exaggerated laughter, but Michael was quiet and motionless, save for one gesture— a quick backwards toss of his lank black hair. At once it settled over his eyes again.

The door at the top of the stairs opened. "Shelley?" called Barb, her voice tired and extra-husky.

"Yes, Mom?" answered Shelley in the purest of tones, gesturing rapidly at the boys to keep silent.

"Time to quiet down, babe. We're gonna turn in. You know Dad's gotta be at the mill before sunrise. You girls get to bed soon, all right? No more fooling around."

"Okay, Mom." The door closed again. Muffled giggles escaped all round.

Troy put his arms around Shelley's shoulders. He indicated the Ouija board with a toss of his head. "Are you playing a game, Shell? I know a quiet game we can all play. How 'bout 'Spin the Bottle?'"

Lisa eagerly drained her Coke and held up the glass vessel.

Michael Joe unzipped his ski jacket for a moment, pulling out half a mickey of Captain Morgan's Dark Rum.

The girls regarded him with awe.

"Where did you get it?" asked Lisa.

"From my uncle."

"Dan Joe? He *gave* it to you?"

Something like anger flickered across Michael's face. "No. 'Course he didn't give it to me. He's not some kinda...he quit drinkin' last week. Threw the bottle in the river," he said, and took a confident swig. "I rescued it." Flicker of a smile.

"You're a hero, Mike," crowed Troy, reaching for the bottle. "Someone should give you a medal."

So Michael Joe had booze, something that promoted them all to the rank of real teenager. And he was really thirteen years old, which helped. Playing Spin the Bottle was probably beneath him, Sappho reflected, just like sandwiches at lunchtime were, and classwork, and anywhere at Gray Star Elementary except for Out Back. For herself and for Ruth, Out Back was simply a hiding-place. But Michael Joe actually seemed to like it there.

Anyway, it was a quiet place to smoke. No teachers ever came to bother them. Now here she was with the Gang in an actual rec room, and no-one (except maybe Lisa) seemed to want to beat her up. Ruth was nowhere to be seen and never would be, Sappho knew, and she felt a pang of guilt. Ruth was absent; Sappho was present. And Michael Joe was there too. He was sitting with all of them in a circle.

Lisa placed her Coke bottle in the centre and gave a careless little laugh, as if to signal that if Troy had been joking, she was in on the joke.

"Spin it," said Claude.

"*Wait*," blurted out Shelley. She stared hard at Troy.

A little debate erupted: since Shelley and Troy were already Going Around, shouldn't they sit this out? And that was the result. They got up and curled up together on the white couch, a real couple.

"Eh, is she in da mood?" asked Claude, snickering. "Better check dat ring."

"Mind your own beeswax, Claude," shot back Troy.

As Lisa spun the bottle, he and Shelley began to neck.

Sappho and Gilles. "Guy-la-Fleur," said Gilles in a deep voice. They both leaned over, and, meeting above the bottle, kissed on the lips. Not so bad. His lips were soft. Everyone screamed with delight.

"Dat's it! You did it, man!" yelled Claude. "Lesbo won't look at no girls no more!"

Sappho blushed so hard she felt like she had a sunburn. But no-one was paying attention. They were yelling at Gilles to spin the bottle, spin it.

Lisa and Michael. Lisa put on a cool expression. Michael looked as unmoved as ever. Lisa flipped her feathered hair back and leaned forward, kissing Michael Joe like she was in a movie, very dramatic. She pulled back to survey the effect. Nothing. His eyes were hidden, his lips immobile. He did have a smear of lip-gloss across them, however. He didn't move to wipe it too fast.

"Whew!" sighed Lisa boldly. "Hot stuff!" She bowed her head and flipped her hair again, sending the feathers flying into place.

"I tink she frenched him, man," remarked Claude.

"Screw. YOU," said Lisa.

"Whoa," Claude howled, shaking his hand as if she'd scalded it.

"*Sssh!*" broke in Shelley. "My folks will hear you."

It was Michael's turn to spin the bottle.

Sappho and Michael Joe.

Claude fell backwards onto the floor and whacked it dramatically. "Oh, man, what about me? Dis bottle don't like me!"

"Aw, it just knows you're a total faggot!" crowed Gilles. The two of them tussled , choking with laughter. Shelley kept shushing them. Sappho and Michael were left to obey the bottle as Lisa looked on, her glare scorching and her arms crossed tightly across her chest.

Now he was sitting on an armchair in a dark part of the room. Obeying a sharp impulse, she made straight for his lap. Someone was playing "Roxy Roller" by Sweeney Todd—over and over. She felt a thrill, as well as something insinuating disaster—social disaster, for somewhere she knew perfectly well that Lisa liked him. And Sappho knew that her own membership in the Gang was flimsy at best. What possessed her? It was him. His gold-toned hands were beautiful. Slender. His lank black hair was vaguely layered, though he made little effort to feather it. He was a *teenager*. He was a really, really cute boy. She knew that now.

They were kissing. His tongue was in her mouth, and Sappho noted to herself that this was french necking. It was her first try. Frenching was startling and kind of gross at first, but she found herself liking it. He tasted like cigarettes as well as rum, smoky-sweet... amazing. Her own skin and hair smelled all cigarette-smoky now too.

They necked for a long time. The lights were down all over the rec room now and Troy and Shelley were necking too. Claude and Gilles were drinking the rest of the booze. Where was Lisa? It seemed private, it seemed concealed there in the dark of the living-room, but of course it wasn't. They were a centrepiece couple high up on their armchair, with potato chips smashed underfoot and strewn around like confetti. Sappho's mouth and chin were raw from rubbing, and everything smelled like tobacco: delicious. She could feel his chest and arms through his ski jacket and shirt and t-shirt. She unzipped the jacket a ways.

At some point he tongued her ear and neck and she felt goosebumps wash over her scalp for the second time that night; she tried it on him and he shivered. They went on like that for two hours. What possessed her? It was him. It was Michael Joe.

"Michael," Sappho said thickly, pulling back. His name sounded strange, unfamiliar. He was like a new person now.

He looked at her from behind his hair.

"Can I ask you something?"

He nodded.

"Why—why—is your uncle ignoring my—Billy?"

Michael maintained his customary silence. Finally he said, "Dan's ignoring all you guys."

That meant white people, obviously. Sappho felt embarrassed. To hide her face, she kissed him again.

Michael put his wet lips close to her wet ear and whispered. "That Billy guy showed Dan some book. A book about Indians. After he read it"—he licked her ear again—"he decided to quit talkin' to all you guys."

After a few more deep kisses, he drew back for air. "My uncle's not the only guy from the Rez who's doin' it," he went on.

"Doing what?"

"Ignorin' you guys. Uncle Dan told a buncha people: don't talk to them others. Don't talk to ghosts, eh? Says it's all a curse or somethin'."

"A curse? But what's that— Billy's not—" Michael shook his black hair back. He placed a finger over her lips. Looking Sappho in the eye, he smiled, something she had rarely seen him do. "Ssshh," he said, tugging her toward him again, closing the gap.

When the boys eventually slipped back out into the dark and she was ducking beneath the fresh linens and downy comfort of Dana's bed, Sappho idled at the threshold of sleep. There, one game merged seamlessly with the next; the Ouija board became a gambling game of chance. The Ouija's message arrived in a bottle, bobbing down the river toward the sea. She crouched by the river's edge and reached for it, almost falling in as a result.

Local Band Faction Employs "Silent Treatment"
by David Mahoney

Gray Star residents expressed puzzlement this week in the face of an apparent "conversation strike" on the part of many local natives. For reasons this reporter is as yet unable to uncover, a significant number of band members have cut off social contact with non-natives, causing widespread confusion and disrupting the tourist industry. Stated Vern Campbell of Snohomish, Washington, a visitor to Gray Star, "I pulled over to ask an Indian lady directions to the beach. She gave me the silent treatment. Just kept walking, acted like I didn't even exist." Similar incidents have been reported all over the area. Lifelong Gray Star resident Linda O'Grady, manager of the SuperStar supermarket, reports a sharp decline in visits from native customers. "Those that do come in won't even pass the time of day," she revealed yesterday. "They just throw down their money and walk out with their purchases. Sometimes they don't take their change, just leave the silver sitting on the counter. Makes you think you've got fleas or something," she added, apparently distraught.

Asked to comment as he left Saturday services at the Temple of St. Zadkiel and Other Archangels on Crowe Road, local chief Raphael Joe blamed a dissident group, but could offer few specifics. "I don't know what those guys are up to now," he said. A devout Angelican, Chief Joe had this to say about tensions building in the community: "The world's upside down. What else is new?"

On Sunday Barb took Sappho to see her mom, who was still living at the StarSpray Motel, waiting for the baby to come. "I'll wait out in the car. You two need to catch up."

Kate was in bed. She held a hand out to Sappho, who took it for a moment before letting it drop. "They change the sheets every day, Sapph. And the SuperStar is just a five-minute walk from here." When Sappho didn't respond, Kate sighed. "When you have a baby yourself one day, you'll understand why I can't be up at Chickenland right now. It's just too crazy." Kate looked away.

"Mom," said Sappho.

"Mmm."

"MOM."

"What *is* it? I'm exhausted."

"WHY did you give me this stupid name?"

"What on Earth—? What stupid name? You should be *proud* to carry the name of a great woman writer!

Honestly! What would you prefer to have been called—Edith?" Billy had a hen called Edith.

"What's wrong with, um, Linda? Or Tracey? Or, or—just anything *normal*?"

"Oh, this is just *great*. JUST what I need right now."

"The kids at school make fun of me! They say mean stuff because of my weird name—and our— and—everything—"

"Well, if you listen to a bunch of narrow-minded twerps at school, you're no better than they are. 'Normal'! I didn't raise you to be *normal*. Where is all this coming from?" But Kate didn't wait for an answer. She curled up in bed with a book, her flannel back to Sappho.

Sappho didn't slam the door—not quite.

Barb dropped her off at Chickenland for a while. "I'll be back after church, hon," she called as she lurched down the rough driveway. "Pack up some more of your school clothes." Sappho turned and faced the A-frame. The afternoon was rainy and dark; the house was dark too. But Billy's truck was there.

The cabin door was half-open. "Billy?" she called as she mounted the steps and looked in. "Finn?" No answer. All Sappho could hear were chickens issuing drawn-out and wary clucks.

She felt for the faithful flashlight standing by the door, the one that had accompanied her into the deep dark night so many times. Turning it on, she swept the beam around the cabin.

The chickens were all over the house.

They were roosting everywhere— along the kitchen counters, on the Singer sewing machine, on chairbacks and bedheads. They had spilled oats and cornmeal on the floor. About ten hens were pecking away down there. The rooster stood on Kate's bureau. White and grey-green chicken crap spattered the whole place. Some of the chickens were looking at her sideways. Warning clucks and squawks came from all directions. The rooster hopped to the ground and advanced on her aggressively.

She turned and, slamming the door behind to prevent the remainder of the flock getting in, she ran down the steps. A latecomer went squawking off in hysterics.

Where were Billy and Finn? Sappho could think of one place only.

Now she noticed that kerosene lamps shone in the windows of the chicken coop. She knocked and turned the doorknob simultaneously, peering around the door. "Hello?" she called softly.

"C'mon in, babe. Ain't nobody here but us," rasped Billy faintly.

He had slung hammocks from the support beams. There they lay, side by side, swinging gently, each swaddled in blankets. Billy was holding a wine bottle, and Finn was nursing some soda pop. There was an empty pizza box on the floor. A pile of books and comics lay there too.

"What're you guys doing in here? The house is full of chickens!"

Billy gave a fond little laugh. "I know, but I... just can't fight them any more, Sapph. They staged a full-scale invasion... and I mean, every time I turned around the damn front door was open again. They kept right on pushing their way across... and I ain't got the heart to keep shooin' them out. They seem so comfortable in there, and I think... who am I to kick them out? What makes me so high 'n' mighty? Wish I knew what was wrong with the doors, though... and windows, come to think of it." He lifted the bottle to his lips. "Anyway, lucky I did all this reno work on the coop... it's pretty darn snug in here. Ain't that right, pardner?" he asked, turning to Finn, who nodded cheerfully.

"Billy, what are you talking about? It's a chicken coop! And those birds are wrecking all our stuff!"

Billy sighed and tugged on his beard. "Aw, they mean well..."

"I moved *my* stuff out here," Finn informed her, pointing to a little collection of clothes and toys piled in the corner. "That way the chickens can't get it."

"Just a minute."

Sappho tramped back to the A-frame. The door was open again for some reason. She stepped noisily over the threshold and flapped her arms fearlessly. Birds squawked angrily and flapped in all directions. She clambered up to the loft and collected some more of her clothes and books. Sappho heard a honk from the driveway: Barb was back. Her arms full of stuff, Sappho stumbled back outside and put her head through the chicken coop door.

"I'll see you guys... later..."

Billy raised his bottle and waggled it.

Sappho ate meatloaf and mashed potatoes at the Taylor dinner table. They had Jello for dessert, which they ate in front of the tv—Sappho, Shelley, Barb, and Mr. Taylor, who had short salt-and-pepper hair and a moustache and wore a plaid shirt, kind of like a man in a cigarette ad. *Happy Days* was on. When it was over, Shelley spent an hour on the phone. Lying on her stomach on the white couch, waving her feet and fiddling with the coiled white phone cord, she laughed and whispered. She didn't say much to Sappho. Later on, tucked into the freshly laundered sheets of Dana's bed, in Dana's room, Sappho pored over his comic-book collection. After a while, Barb tapped at the door. She came and sat on the bed. She was wearing quite a fancy white nightie and bathrobe set, together with fluffy powder-blue slippers. Sappho guessed she was thinking of all the nights she had looked in on her son as he grew, sat on his bed, kissed him and wished him sweet dreams. Now Barb smiled and kissed Sappho. "It's late," she said. "Turn off the light soon. And hon? Don't mind Shelley. Her manners aren't great. We spoiled her some over the last few years." Then she left the room. The carpeting seemed to muffle everything in the Taylor house, Sappho reflected. She turned off the bedside lamp.

She thought of Billy and Finn in their hammocks, the chickens roosting in the A-frame, and Kate in her motel-room, curled around her baby as they waited. The baby floated within, safe again; salty. Sappho thought it would be like being in the sea, like snorkeling maybe. That's what she would use next summer when she played mermaid once more. A snorkel. Now she was peering at the undersea world... surfacing to see the sky again...

Sappho closed her eyes and the Salmon Princess opened hers.

She blinked. She couldn't believe what she saw. Those Others were still there, most of them bobbing around in the river.

He was still standing there with his hand extended, and his hand was full of those scales, the biggest and shiniest fish-scales she had ever seen or imagined. They were patterned too, and she longed to pore over them. His sea-coloured eyes looked into hers, full of meaning. You are the Salmon Princess, they seemed to say. These are a fit offering for you from the Other world, where the fish grow huge and strange.

The Salmon Princess knew that nothing from the Other world should pass over and remain. But the scales belonged to her— she was the Salmon Princess, and she yearned to take possession. Even as she reached for them, she felt a pang of fear and heard voices whisper of dark danger ahead. The Other stretched out his hands and she mimed him. The scales fell onto her palms with a weird kind of music. They were harder than anything, maybe even stone. They were heavy. Even so, the Salmon Princess could not mask her glee. She smiled, she laughed; the Other did the same.

The next day at school was one of the worst ever. The Girls Gang ignored Sappho completely at recess, standing with their denim backs ranked against her in one corner of the blacktop. Her brand-new Gang membership had been cancelled. As she passed the group, she saw Lisa toss her feathers back and look over her shoulder, lips twisted. She got back to her desk to find that someone had scratched "the Lesbo is a slut" on its surface.

At lunchtime, Sappho was on her way to her old hiding place Out Back when Lisa suddenly appeared flanked by two other girls from their class. Lisa gave her a push.

"I know why you're goin' Out Back, Lesbo Joe," she said in her cold way. "You slut. I oughtta kick your head in and teach you a lesson."

Sappho stood frozen, avoiding Lisa's eyes. Lisa grabbed hold of Sappho's jean jacket, shook her, and sent her flying backwards. She landed in the gravel. Lisa laughed and walked away. "You better watch yourself," she yelled. "Indian lover."

Michael Joe wasn't Out Back, but Ruth was. She had several issues of *Tiger Beat* stashed out there somehow. Wrapped in a plastic bag and stuck under a rock? Ruth seemed hesitant to talk to Sappho, as though this wild bout of unpopularity might be catching, but she did pass on one of the magazines. Sappho felt too sick with misery to eat anything Barb had packed her, except for the chocolate pudding. She passed the rest of the hour in silence, trying to read an article about Leif Garrett's idea of the perfect girl. The perfect girl would like Leif for himself. Looks weren't so important, though he did like blue eyes, he said. Leif was a "real" kind of boy, not into Hollywood games or fakeness or anything. That was the gist of it.

Shelley wasn't much help. Sappho knew Shelley could rescue her easily, but she didn't seem to want to. After Barb drove them home, Sappho made straight for Dana's bedroom. She could hear Shelley laughing and whispering on the phone again.

Later Sappho ran into her on her way to the bathroom.

"Lisa wants to kill you," she said calmly.

"Why?" returned Sappho, though she thought she could guess.

"She liked Michael. You knew that. Everyone knew that."

Sappho had known that, it was true. "They weren't Going Around," she offered helplessly.

Shelley shrugged and closed her eyes. Sappho could see nothing but pale blue frosted eye-shadow and mascara'd lashes. "So? They would have been, prob'ly."

If Sappho hadn't sat in his lap. If Sappho, the slut, hadn't spent hours in his lap french-necking. Who knew what Michael Joe would say about any of this? But it wouldn't make any difference to Lisa.

Sappho's popularity was over before it had really begun.

Lying in bed that night, Sappho felt the black night

pushing in at the windows like floodwaters. She heard the cedars scratch the windows. Bits of cold sweat kept appearing in her eyebrows, and she kept wiping until finally she fell into a troubled sleep.

Trouble: there was no other way to describe the manifestation of Others at the mouth of the river. Now the Salmon Princess' hands were bulging with the huge fish scales, and the Other seemed to want something in return. He did not touch her, luckily. No, he mystified her by producing some enormous leaves—or perhaps pieces of bark?—which were scored with whorling lines, lines which the Other kept tracing with his finger as he stared into her eyes and jabbered on in his incomprehensible tongue. By this time, some of the other Salmon Clan members had arrived, trying to mask their terror with blank faces. The Salmon Princess hid her hands in the folds of her cloak. The enchanted fish-scales belonged to her alone. No-one else would have them.

Then two of the Others approached bearing a new gift. The first Salmon Man frowned and tried to shoo them away, but the second and the third were tempted. The Others, trickster types, were laughing and dancing away out of reach. Eventually they gave the clan members some strange bags, leathery things that turned out to contain some kind of dark water. It smelled sweet and strong, like stewed berries— and something else. It smelled like trouble. Some of the clan members began sipping it. The Salmon Princess knew that accepting Other material went against countless warnings." Don't drink it," she commanded, echoing those lessons, but the people paid no attention. They drank. What could she do? She herself had already accepted an Other gift, and if she tried to stop them drinking, tried to block them with her body—words had no effect— her scales would shower to the ground for all to see. They kept drinking. Unearthly joy seemed to rise in them.

The Other with the huge leaves kept pointing to the lines etched there, his voice full of questions. First he caressed the lines with a finger. Then, for some reason, he pointed outwards at the ocean, waving his finger this way and that. He indicated the sea; he indicated the lines. He started jabbing his finger in one spot, then another. He jabbed one spot with special intensity. It was confusing. The Salmon Princess, experimentally, jabbed her finger there too, and this seemed to satisfy, to delight him actually. He ran off back towards the impossibly big boat. The Salmon Princess could now think only of hiding her tribute somewhere, keeping it safe from the other Salmon People. After all, though she was the princess, they might decide that the fantastical fish-scales were meant for the whole Salmon clan. She couldn't bear that idea. She stole away into the forest and concealed them among the mossy roots of a favourite spruce tree.

Chapter Seven

Sappho's early morning fears ebbed when she remembered it was Saturday. There would be no school, thankfully— two days free from the rest of the kids. Even the youngest had heard the news that Lesbo was a slut, and wherever she went she was dogged by chants and promises heavy with menace. *Hey Lesbo, see you after school.* Mr. Mahoney, oblivious as usual, smiled at her and asked her sunnily how she was, confident of the answer. *Uhh, okay I guess. Super!* he replied. Between her and the safety of his world there seemed to lie a solid foot of glass. Sappho pictured herself in an aquarium, trying to speak and sending up nothing but bubbles. "Super!" said her teacher again, and turned his attention elsewhere.

Some part of a nightmare lingered. Water again— and the sodden pillow-case. She was on the riverbank gazing upon the rushing water, trying to see something.

Her reflection? How could she use the rushing river like a mirror? Its surface was whorled with all the textures of the current. But for a brief moment it lay still and smooth. Behind the image of a girl, something flashed metallic. It looked like fish. And something awful—a mermaid shedding scales, leaking blood into the river. Sleep offered little refuge these days.

Sappho thought of school again. She thought of the other kids, and wished she did not have to face them even one more time. Anyway, two full days of freedom lay ahead. She would have liked to watch Saturday morning cartoons, a rare treat, but she had to get out of the house before Shelley got up and – horror of horrors—invited Lisa over. No, she would make her way to Chickenland and see Billy. She got up and pulled on her jeans and t-shirt. She padded upstairs and went into the kitchen.

Barb was at the kitchen table, smoking and drinking coffee. "Hey, sweetheart," said Barb, and blew a smoke ring. "How're you doin' today?" Sappho so liked the friendly creases around her eyes, her lightly raspy voice. If only she could spend all her time with adults, Sappho felt, she would be happy. She dreamed of doing correspondence, of never having to venture down the school halls again, never having to run that gauntlet again.

"Hon, let me tell you something. I threw that damn Ouija board in the garbage. No—don't say a word. A mother knows, eh? That thing is just bad news. How can I put it? You call ghosts into your life, they come runnin'. Open the door a crack, they come bustin' in. Not so easy to get rid of 'em."

Sappho nodded.

Barb gave her a quick hug. Then she made her guest a bowl of Frosted Flakes. "Any plans for today?" she asked, as Sappho munched away.

"I'd like to go to the cabin again," Sappho replied. "And see Billy."

"I'll run you up," she said, taking a long drag on her cigarette, blowing the smoke sideways.

The A-frame didn't smell like people at all any more, just chickens. Sappho had to wade her way through the whole flock to get to the rope-ladder. She hastily gathered up some more of her things, made her way down and out again. She walked over to the coop and tapped.

"C'mon in," she heard Billy croak.

She found Billy and Finn clustered around a Bunsen burner. They seemed to be wearing every sweater and jacket they owned.

"We're making Campbell's soup," explained Finn with a contented air.

"Scotch Broth," added Billy.

"Billy," said Sappho. He turned to look at her, his blue eyes sad and a little bloodshot.

"Yeah, kid?" She had never heard him sound so tired.

"Are you just going to go on living here in the coop?"

"Why not? I spent the last two years fixing it up nice. *Someone* oughtta enjoy it."

"Billy..."

"I spent the last two years fixing it up for those damn birds, and they don't appreciate it. I worked my ass off to make the A-frame comfy for your mother, and she's taken up residence at the StarSpray Motel. I spent years working with Dan Joe, excavating in and around the midden, and we found all kindsa things for their collection. I spent ages researching stories the whole fucking tribe had apparently managed to forget. Yep, they needed ME to get that stuff, and now Dan of all people can't be bothered to speak to me! It's like, it's like... *he doesn't even know I exist,*" Billy said in a funny girlish vice, and gave a little snort. "Why the hell shouldn't I stay in this chicken coop?"

"Did you show Dan Joe a book? About Indians, I mean?"

"Among other things," Billy replied, and laughed a bitter laugh. "Yeah. Weobrun's *Prominent Myths.* You know the one. I was *trying* to read it to your mother on Hallowe'en. Dan and I used to talk all the time, read stuff, toss ideas around...until that time I saw him down by the General Store. That bastard hasn't seen fit to acknowledge my ass from that day to this. When I think of all the... of everything I did, all the good times we had, it just makes me wanna..."

"I know, Billy, but it's not just you he's ignoring," Sappho broke in. "He won't talk to any white people now, and neither will lots of the Indians. Michael says after he read the book you gave him, he threw a bottle of booze in the river. Then he told everyone on the Rez not to talk to ghosts. He means us. He says we're like a curse or something."

Billy snorted again. "Well, sure, that's what I was tryin' to tell your mother. And there's somethin' in it. I don't really blame them. But how come I get lumped in? I mean, after all I did for those guys... you'd think I'd merit some kinda..."

He laughed angrily some more, but then he stopped. When he spoke again, his tone had changed. "A curse? The kid used that exact word?"

He jumped up when she nodded.

"Lemme find that book." Off he strode to the A-frame. Sappho felt a wavelet of relief. Billy was acting a bit more like Billy at last. She followed him, and Finn followed her.

After a few minutes poring over the book, Billy got out some notepaper began and jotting fast. "Okay, let's get this show on the road. Weoburn mentions a legendary ship and some precious metal. That could be Sir Francis

Drake and his guys, right? The local Natives take them for a bunch of ghosts or fairies, like the book says. These guys lay some silver or gold—Spanish coins, maybe; stuff they looted—on the Indians. The Englishmen want something— the keys to the Northwest Passage, probably. One way or another, they raise hell; everything's screwed up after that. Michael says there's a curse— maybe, instead of the vague thing I had in mind, it's specific. Specific to the stuff Drake left here. Let's say it's coins. Blood money.

"I've been fiddling around the midden for years. We've found lots of great native stuff, but nothing remotely European. Forget it— coins aren't going to be at the midden. We ain't gonna find this treasure at the town dump. But where the hell are they?"

The huge spectral boat had vanished. It had gone, but all was not well. Something terrible had happened to the Salmon People. The boat had gone as suddenly as it had arrived—the Salmon Princess had no way of knowing where, whether back below the river or out into the sea—and it had taken something priceless away with it. She had never seen her people look so bad or behave so disturbingly. It was early morning, and some of the men were ranting, wild, while others had collapsed on the ground and lay deep in an unwholesome sleep. They mumbled and rolled in the dirt. Some were on their hands and knees, vomiting. The ones who could talk blamed the dark water the Others had brought— it was burning water, water which did not slake thirst but only inflamed it.

The Salmon Princess knew better.

The next morning, things were worse. Several babies and two of the older children had red spots on their faces and bodies. They were hot to the touch, hot. Their breath came in thick pants. They sweated and groaned in their mothers' arms. The children seemed close to death.

The Salmon Princess knew why the people were sick: it was her fault. She had been the one, the first one, to accept a gift from the Others. All her life she had been warned against doing this very thing, and she had done it. The Others are clever, she had heard. They will offer things that seem to call you by name. The Others had come directly to her. They had only had to try her, the Salmon Princess, one time—and she had fallen. She, who should have been strong, was fatally weak. Thanks to her weakness, all of her people were dying. The world was poisoned.

The Salmon Princess was filled with shame. Seawater tears ran down her cheeks. Already the solution was obvious. She had to return the terrible gift. She would carry it back to the Others and restore her people as best she could. She could only hope it would be enough—even now, thanks to her frailty, the boat full of Others was might well be loose in the world wreaking havoc.

She could do one thing only: return the monstrous scales to the threshold beneath the river, the place upstream where the wall between human and Other realms grew thin, perforated. No-one disagreed with her. Not one of the elders she spoke to in the longhouse that day expressed surprise or even dismay. The Others had acted the way they had always been rumoured to act, and a human being had fallen into their snares, placing the whole human world at risk. The disaster did not shock them, and neither did the solution proposed by the Salmon Princess.

Some of the elders accompanied her to the hiding-place near the river, and for this she was grateful, as the scales were beautiful and hard to resist. The elders followed her to the river's edge in silence, then melted away, back into the forest. The Salmon Princess stood alone on the riverbank. She took off most of her garments—they were heavy—and wrapped the wretched scales in a piece of hide. They would be easier to carry that way, and she feared lest one or more slip through her fingers as she swam. Not one scale should remain among human beings; they must all be returned to the Other realm. Without ceremony the Salmon Princess waded into the water and began the difficult task of swimming upriver carrying her burden.

The river ran hard towards the sea, and she made slow progress. It was hard to swim while carrying the pouch. Up, up she pushed towards the place where the Otherworld yawned. She kept surfacing for air, but more than once found her mouth and nose filled with water. Still furiously beating her legs and free arm against the force of the water, she kept swimming, sometimes crying out in fear and frustration, her salt tears lost in the rushing river. The water was getting sweeter, though—she could taste it. When she reached the place where the worlds met she tread water with all her strength. And then she dove.

Beneath the river the Salmon Princess opened her eyes. She could see rocks in a heap. Rolled away, they would reveal a gaping tunnel to the Other side. But if she did find the strength to open that door, what would happen? Would more of the Others make their way into her world? The Salmon Princess could leave the terrible scales there at the threshold, under a rock; surely the Others would retrieve them, take them back them to their hoard. Anyway, with her strength fading, it was all she could do. The Salmon Princess dove again. She took hold of a craggy rock, clung to it, pulled. Failing to budge it, she rose to the surface to breathe, then went down once more. Once again she took hold of the sharp slippery rock that lay between herself, her world, and the Others. Her fingers were raw, torn up; there was blood in the water. Finally, drawing on her last reserves of power, churning her limbs against the relentless hard tug towards the ocean, the Salmon Princess managed to dislodge the stone. Her hands were shredded, the water cloudy with red. She tucked the pouch into the riverbed and began hauling the stone back on top of it, fearful of what pale inquisitive faces might push out, what pale hair waving like seaweed, what white arms might snake out from below. Now at last the stone was in place, the tainted treasure returned. She gave thanks. Exhausted, she relaxed and stopped fighting the current. It bore her away from the Others, and fear left her. It was done. It was finished.

Now, as her body floated rapidly back to the sea, the Salmon Princess began to breathe water.

Once he got going, it didn't take Billy too long to round up the indignant chickens and show them the door. Driving the last stragglers before him, he left the A-frame with the children and went out to the truck. The truck

coughed and hacked, taking some minutes to ignite—
"it's been, what, ten days since we fired 'er up, buddy?"
Finn nodded. They waited as Billy revved the gas, warming the engine. "We'll clean the cabin later," he added.
"Right now, we got business to take care of." But just as
he started to back out, the woods began to whine. It was
the Volunteer Fire Department calling.

"Oh, Lordy—just what we need now. Another drill or
something. Last time, we were trying to torch some old
condemned cabin so we could put it out for practice.
But it was raining so damn hard—we never could get
the thing to catch fire. The rain kept snuffing it out."
But Billy dutifully ran back to the house for his boots
and yellow slicker. He tossed some grain at the evicted
chickens. "Better head over to the Department and see
what's what."

They made their way to the end of the driveway and
turned left. Then they passed the fire truck speeding
noisily in the opposite direction. T.J., the town Zamboni
driver, was at the wheel. Various figures hung off its sides,
waving at them. Billy pulled a U-turn and took off after
them. "Looks like we might have an actual fire this time,"
he said. "Yah!" cried Finn.

They clattered over the bridge. Soon after that, they
saw Cowboy Cal's rainbow-festooned truck speeding un-

steadily towards them. "Where does he think he's going? Cal's on the volunteer team," said Billy.

"I think I saw my mom in there," Finn put in quietly. "Driving."

"Me too," added Sappho. What she had seen looked like Cal trying to wrestle the wheel away from Nancy.

A loud tearing noise came from the direction of the bridge. But there was no time to investigate. Just at that minute, they sighted the Goon Saloon. Smoke was pouring out of all its crevices and flames darted out the windows. More mechanical wailing—for a moment it seemed to Sappho that a choir of sirens filled the air, with voices howling from all directions.

Billy pulled over. "You kids stay in here," he said firmly. "I mean it. Stay away from the fire." He got out, slammed the door, and, pulling on his gear, ran towards the shiny red fire engine. Sappho and Finn watched and worried as Billy and seven other men in gumboots uncoiled a massive hose.

"Turn 'er on!" called Billy, and they pointed the jet of water into the saloon windows.

Bob's black dog was barking wildly.

"Where's Bob?" yelled T.J. "We better get in there." But just at this moment, Blow-Yer-Brains-Out Bob came staggering out the front door, holding a stubby brown beer bottle. The firemen cheered. Coughing and a bit singed, Bob toasted them. He had cheated death once more.

"Is anyone else in there, Bob?" asked T.J.

"Well... I don't see Cal's truck. I think him and his ol' lady were crashed out on the couch."

"We saw them tearing down the highway on our way here," panted Billy, gripping the snaking hose.

"Man, that's freaky," remarked Bob. "Bottoms up," he added, and drained his beer.

Still coughing, he wove his way across the street accompanied by his dog and sat down on the steps of the General Store to watch the proceedings.

"Wonder where the cops are?" said Bob at one point. "They never like to miss any action at the ol' Goon Saloon." The firemen struggled on. "I should like maybe call the cop-shop," Bob added.

The fire was out. The exhausted volunteers rolled up the hose and boarded the truck, with the exception of Billy, who got back into his pickup and gave each of the kids a tight hug. He was wet and smelled of cinders. The fire truck pulled away, and they followed it.

As they approached the river, traffic slowed. Something was blocking the road. They got out and climbed up on the truck to get a look. A bizarre scene was unfolding. The RCMP cruiser was parked on the bridge, lights flashing. A crowd had gathered. The rails of the bridge were torn away. In the river, its cab just visible above the rushing waters, was Cowboy Cal's pickup. "Oh hell," said Billy tensely, pulling in behind the fire truck. Everyone jumped out and ran up to join the crowd.

Officers Macleod and Stivitch had left their boots, hats, and gun-belts on the bridge and were in the river, clinging to the truck, trying to open the doors. Sappho could see arms sticking out the windows, one of them straining to hold a guitar above water. She could also see that the water was rising as the truck sank. "Mom!" called Finn, pitching forward; Sappho held him back, wrapping her arms around him. Within seconds, the Volunteer Fire Department were stripped down to their long underwear and jumping into the river.

A truck from Dave's Towing and Salvage arrived.

Now it seemed like half of Gray Star was there. Sappho heard the frustrated honking of cars trying to make it to the ferry, and saw other drivers leave their cars and join the onlookers. She saw Michael Joe and his uncle in the crowd. She saw Chief Raphael. She waved to Barb, who blew her a kiss. Now the crowd seemed to sigh with relief—"What's going on?" whimpered Finn, and Sappho lifted him up in time to witness Officer Macleod pull Nancy from the truck and, gripping her voluminous blue dress, begin to pull her to the river bank. A minute later, Billy got ahold of Cowboy Cal, who still had the guitar aloft, though his ten-gallon hat was floating away, under the bridge and out to sea. They reached the river-bank and climbed it. After a while, Billy came huffing up to reassure the kids. This time his embrace was sodden.

Now Michael Joe was standing next to them. "Hey," he said.

"Hi," replied Sappho. She scrambled for something more to say. "Um, Dana's car landed in the same place, didn't it? That's weird."

"It's not so weird."

She turned to look at him, calm as ever behind his black hair.

"Not if you ask my grandpa, it isn't," he added.

"What do you mean?" put in Billy.

"Well, he's right over there. Get him to tell you. Hey, Gramps!" Chief Raphael turned around, his long grey braid swinging. "These guys are asking about all the accidents here on the bridge."

Chief Raphael sighed. "That place in the river there— it's like a... doorway. Trouble magnet, eh? All kinds a no good goes on here. Always has."

"Why didn't you guys mention this before?" asked Billy.

"You asked to dig the midden," said the Chief, shrugging. "You never asked nothin' about the river."

Billy laughed cheerfully.

Sappho closed her eyes for a minute. When she opened them, both Michael Joe and the Chief had vanished.

The Mounties were talking to Nancy and Cal. All four of them were wrapped in striped wool blankets courtesy of the Volunteer Fire Department. Cal wore his like a hood, concealing his naked head and enfolding his guitar. Billy walked over to join them, and the kids, hand-in-hand, followed along.

He pointed at the drenched woman. "Hey, the cops netted the mer-monster at last!"

"Hil—*ar*-ious," responded Nancy flatly. She didn't look at Finn.

"As I was saying then, you two seem to have fled the scene of a fire, if our information is correct." Officer Macleod paused and, getting no reaction, he folded his black rubber arms and continued. "Can you explain your conduct?"

Cowboy Cal, smoking a rollie someone had fixed him, stared at the ground. Nancy stuck her hands on her hips and tossed her wet hair. "We escaped with our *lives*, 'Officer'! Is that a crime?"

"Well, yes, possibly. Ma'am, if either of you is responsible for sparking that blaze—and then fleeing the scene—yes. And then there is the question of Mr. Bob

Dobson, who, as you know, lives down below. You failed to alert him to the danger. Fortunately, he survived."

"Don't you dare lay a guilt-trip on me, *man*. I refuse to take that on."

Billy put his hands on Cal's slumped shoulders. Cal looked miserable. "Cal, you're a volunteer fireman! Why the hell were you driving *away* from the scene?"

Nancy smirked. "Isn't it obvious? He was embarrassed. He passed out with a smoke in his mouth and set the couch on fire! What a cretin."

Cowboy Cal flinched. "You don't know that for sure," he said softly.

Nancy laughed. "Know what—that you set the couch on fire, or that you're a cretin?"

"She took off in my truck, Billy," Cal said, his voice becoming high and trembly. "All my gear's in the back—even my big fire extinguisher."

"Be qui-et, Cal," sang Nancy.

"She–she was takin' off! I grabbed my Gibson and jumped on the running board as she was pulling away... I was trying to get the wheel away from her! We were tussling—we got to the bridge—and all of a sudden, we were through the guard-rail and into the drink! Where... where were you headed?" he asked Nancy, his voice wavering.

She said nothing.

Billy put an arm around his shoulders. "Cal, old buddy, you have *got* to get your act together. First of all, you need a new place to lay your head—know what I mean? Later we'll see about some wheels," he said, jerking his thumb over at the river. "This truck's a write-off."

Nancy cleared her throat. "EXCUSE ME. I DEMAND the recovery of my belongings. I had several valuable items in that stupid truck."

"Well, ma'am, I hope your belongings are waterproof," put in Officer Stivitch.

Billy was pinching his temples. "Good plan, Nancy. I couldn't agree more. Let's pull out the truck first and then salvage what we can before the stuff gets too far downstream." He thought for a moment. "We've got the towtruck. Between all of us, firemen and frogmen and diggers, it shouldn't take too long."

Officer Macleod donned a frog-suit and waded into the river, leaving his partner to drive Nancy and Cal to the RCMP detachment for further questioning.

Chapter Eight

"**N**ow that we've got all that sorted out—Billy, get up!" laughed Kate weakly. "Of course I'll marry you."

Sappho clapped. Once more they were gathered around a sterile hospital bed with Kate in it, her skin white with exhaustion. This time, though, a new baby girl whose hair was as fluffy and wispy as a gosling's lay in the nest of her arms. In all the confusion, all the wails and howls, they had failed to notice the whoop of the ambulance.

Billy stood, bent over, kissed Kate on the lips and stroked the baby's tender head. He felt around in his pocket and extracted something. "This'll have to do for now," he said, taking Kate's hand. "I whittled it for ya."

The ring was incredibly delicate for something made of wood, local arbutus engraved with tiny leaves and flowers and polished to a high shine. Billy slipped it on her ring finger. "Next time round, Katie, you're gonna draw the gold one."

"This one's beautiful, Billy," she said. "I don't need more than this." She turned it around on her finger, following the tiny vines to where they burst into bloom.

"Quick, before our boy gets back from the ice-cream machine—I just want to say that *I'm sorry* I danced around the fact that he's my kid. I thought... I thought it might scare you off. I kept planning to, but things were getting really out of hand with his mother, and..."

"I knew," said Kate. "I knew right away."

"Didja? Yeah, I guess you did. Well, now's the time for me to make it up to him."

Finn came back, his lips stained Popsicle-red. He hovered at the threshold as though he sensed grown-up talk in the offing.

Billy spread his arms. "C'mere, kid. We got some good news." Finn ran to hug him. "To celebrate the arrival of your lovely baby sister here, Kate and I are gonna get married. And we'll need you and Sappho to help us plan the party."

Finn smiled. He looked at the baby who had woven them all together. "What are we going to *name* my baby sister?"

"I thought we would let Sappho choose the name," said Kate. "So I asked her to think about it."

Sappho took a deep breath. "Okay, what about *Alice?* Like the girl in the book."

Kate hummed, considering the name from various angles. "I like it."

"Perfect," said Billy, "Alice it is. And now we'll let you and Alice get some sleep. I've gotta take my team here back to the river."

Kate closed her eyes, sighing with contentment.

On the way out, Sappho asked for a dime and called Mrs. Taylor— Barb—Barb, her best friend—from a payphone to tell her all the news.

"Sweetheart, I am *so* happy for you and your family. Things are lookin' up, eh? I'll drop by the hospital tomorrow and look in on mother and baby."

They arrived back at the rushing river to find Cowboy Cal's truck half-towed from the water. "This is the tricky part," Officer Macleod told them, still in his slick black frog-suit. "Part of the back end is stuck between two big rocks. I've been down to take a look. It's wedged in there real tight. Saw something similar a few years back—the time we lost the Taylor boy. Terrible thing."

"Dana," murmured Sappho. "His Mustang was stuck."

"You got it, young lady. Took us a good while to pry the fender loose. Same spot, same rocks."

The tow-truck accelerated, its wheels spinning in the mud. The sound of tearing metal could be heard. The tow-truck braked.

"Wait up. Can we get us a backhoe?" called Billy.

"Can't hurt," replied Officer Macleod, and flippered over to the police car to use the radio.

Bushy-haired Maureen was passing out sandwiches and hot chocolate to everyone. "The saloon's outta commission again," she said. "Gotta keep busy."

Mel the backhoe guy arrived with his machine, and a tricky hour followed. The whole crew— Officer Macleod, Billy and the rest of the Volunteer Fire Department, Dave the tow-truck driver and assorted onlookers—cleared the riverbank of brush and alder saplings so that the backhoe could get in as close to the spot as possible. They worked fast: the dark was coming down. From her position on the bridge, Sappho glimpsed a lone watcher on the opposite bank. It was Dan Joe, leaning against a tree.

"Okay," yelled Billy. "Good work, everyone. Now what we wanna do is fire up the backhoe and dislodge those two big rocks underwater. Once we get some movement down below, Dave here will give Cal's wheels another tug. That should do it."

Billy's plan worked. As the rainbow-painted pickup emerged from the river streaming water from the cab, the workers gave a fatigued round of applause.

"One more thing," Billy called to Mel. "Scoop me up those rocks and a good foot or two of whatever's underneath. Make it a big scoop."

"Why, for the love of Pete?" he called back.

"Just humour me, willya? There's a two-four in it for ya—or a twenty-sixer a whisky, whatever ya drink. Just dump all the mud and rocks in my front yard."

With a roar the backhoe pulled out a huge scoop—the big gray rocks and a lot of smaller ones, dark mud and pale sand mixed—and pulled back out onto the highway. "I hope to hell it's enough," murmured Billy.

"I'll meet you all back at the firehall for beers and pizza," he told the crew. "Just give me half an hour. I've gotta get this mud home safely—and these kids to bed."

Billy, Sappho and Finn hopped in their truck and followed Mel and his backhoe to Chickenland.

The A-frame was chicken-free, but still fantastically messy. Luckily, the birds hadn't advanced as far as the loft. "That's *another* adorable thing about chickens," observed Billy Black. "They can't flippin' fly!" The kids got into bed. Sleep rapidly smoothed over the turbulence of the day.

Awoken as usual by the rooster crowing, Sappho looked out the picture window. The wind was up, making the cedar branches dance. Between the coop and the cabin lay a shiny blue heap. She squinted, then realized what she was looking at: Billy had thrown a bright tarp over the mound of mud they had lifted from the riverbed.

Downstairs, he was on a cleaning binge, mopping, sweeping and dusting all the chicken droppings and feathers, as well as the oatmeal and cornmeal they had pecked their way into and spread around the place.

"You kids up? I've already been down to Gray Star General.We gotta get this place spic 'n' span for Kate and the baby. They'll be home any day now," he called, his voice brimming with excitement. "Once we've done that, we can resume the treasure-hunt."

So once they had done that, and the A-frame had been restored, and Billy had initiated the elaborate process which would, with luck, result in fresh bedclothes by the end of the day, they sat down to a pancake breakfast. And Billy explained how they would tackle the pile of stones and sludge awaiting them. "Basically we have to pick through the lot. Sift the sand through and keep what's left. Most of it'll be pebbles, but if we're lucky, some thing or things'll be man-made. Keep in mind, this stuff could have been in the river a helluva long time— like centuries— so looks could be deceiving. Okay, let's get started!"

They hurried outside. Billy cobbled together three wooden frames and stretched fine acrylic netting across each of them. He produced three spades, unveiled the mound, and they got to work.

Two hours passed. They had a wide array of sticks and stones fanned out on the blue tarp. Billy sifted and inspected, sifted and inspected. Sappho had turned up some very nicely worn down pieces of frosty blue and green glass for her collection, as well as various other interesting bits.

She was just about to suggest a tea break when Finn announced that he had found a sand-dollar.

"Can sand-dollars *live* in fresh water?" she asked, coming over to have a look. "It's not very big." The sand-dollar, or whatever it was, was black and had uneven edges.

"Lemme have a look, son," said Billy. He palmed the object, held it close to his eyes, and ran his fingers over it. Then he bit it. "Ouch! That's what we want to feel. Pain! Finn, my boy, that is metal. Gen-u-ine silver, I bet! Old silver!" He grabbed Finn and spun him in a joyous circle while Finn screamed with glee. Then, hugging both kids to him, Billy crowed like a rooster.

"I've got a GOOD feeling about this!"

"Let's keep looking. She left more than one."

"Who did, Sapphie?"

"I just... I just remember. Like in a dream. She... she had a handful of them."

"Who'm I to argue?" enthused Billy, attacking the mound with fresh force. "Let's find the rest!"

Within an hour they had recovered twelve of the blackened silver coins. Billy poured them into Sappho's cupped hands, filling them neatly. She felt their weight. She closed her eyes.

"I think that's it," said Sappho Smith. "That's all."

"Well, I'll be a son-of-a-gun. You two are about the best damn archaeological team I've ever worked with."

They went inside for lunch. While the kids ate, Billy rooted around in the cupboards and found some silver polish. "I'll try it with one," he said. "Don't wanna mess with them too much." The polishing took a long time. But as he worked, the thick tarnish gradually paled to reveal patterns on the coin. The first thing they saw was a cross which quartered the coin's surface.

"Yep, this is a Spanish coin all right!" cried Billy. "They called the gold ones *cruzados*. The silver ones, they're eight *reales* each. Pieces of eight, me hearties—pieces of eight!"

He lit a candle and inspected the coin more closely. He turned it over and read some letters aloud. "H-I-S-P-A-N E-T I-N-D-E. It's Latin."

"English pirates *lusted* after these things. If I'm right, and this dates to the sixteenth century, it woulda come out of one of two huge mining operations—one in Mexico City, or another in Bolivia. That was going great guns all through the 1500s, and it petered out in the 1600s. The Spanish were sending these babies to the coast and out by the boatload, and Drake for one loved to pick off those ships." He was still rubbing the coin. Now four hazy heraldic shapes began to appear in its quadrants.

"That looks like a lion," said Sappho.

"I think you're right."

Finn raised his head. "Someone's driving up," he said, and ran to the window to look out. "It's the police car!"

They went outside.

The RCMP cruiser braked sharply to avoid a cluster of chickens. Three men emerged: Officers Macleod and Stivitch, as well as a bedraggled figure wearing a John Deere cap. "Cowboy Cal!" called Billy. "Didn't recognize ya without the usual headgear."

"Yeah, I gotta save up for a new hat," replied Cal, looking dejected. "Somehow."

"Well, between the Mounties here and the folks down at the Stables, we should be able to find ya one. So, what's goin' on? What brings you-all up here?"

Now all three of the visitors looked dejected.

"Well," said Officer Stivitch slowly, "we're seeking the whereabouts of Nancy Hackett."

"Hey, son, will ya go and find me my pipe?" Finn went. Then Billy turned back to the men. "What's goin' on?"

It emerged that Nancy had managed to get ahold of a police revolver. Officer Macleod had returned from the river to find his holster was empty. He rushed back to the police station to find his partner and Cowboy Cal in the lockup. By that time, Nancy had been gone four hours.

"She probably picked it out of my holster after I changed into the frog-suit," blurted out a tomato-faced Officer Macleod, stroking his luxuriant dark brown moustache. "My holster was just lying there on the bridge."

"Don't blame yourself, Doug. She did it right under my nose."

"Does she still *have* the gun?" Billy interjected.

"Uh, no, actually," said Officer Stivitch. "Though she does have some cash from my wallet," he admitted, patting his back pocket. "Once she... locked us up... she made me toss out my gun and the money. Said she'd blow a hole in Cal otherwise. I complied, and she... just tossed the guns on the desk. Said she didn't even *need* a gun anymore."

"Oh, well, *that's* something, anyway."

"*Laughing*," added Cal gloomily. "She laughed at us."

"Well, I'll be damned. At least she wasn't fillin' you fulla holes! Go on along and check out her place if you want, but something tells me she ain't there," said Billy, his voice dropping to a whisper as Finn returned with the pipe.

Off they trooped down the path towards Nancy's house. They rematerialized in the clearing about twenty minutes later, shaking their heads.

Billy softly told Sappho he bet Nancy had hitched her way over the U.S. border by now. "That is one persuasive woman," he said. "Long-haired Nancy in a damp blue gown? Truckers'll be vying for the honour of sneaking her over the border. Bet they'd get her to Argentina if she asked nicely. In fat, that sounds pretty plausible..."

"Hey, officers," he called, as they approached, "why don't you leave Cal with us? He's got nowhere to crash. And he looks like he could use some food and rest." The Mounties looked at each other and seemed to reach an agreement.

"He'll be here if we need to enquire further into the circumstances of the fire?" asked Officer Macleod.

"Sure will."

"I don't see any problem then."

"Thanks, man," said Cowboy Cal, retrieving his guitar from the back seat of the police cruiser. They watched the Mounties pull away. "Anything I can do to help, just say the word." He sat down heavily beside them on the porch.

"Well, since you mention it...are you good with chickens, Cal? Would you call yourself a chicken person? I gotta feeling we'll be needin' someone to look after them soon."

"No problem, man."

"Just keep an eye out. These birds can be hell on wheels."

"You see, Billy? I told you she's sensitive."

"Ain't *that* the truth."

Kate was holding Sappho's little moon-face in her hands and pushing the hair out of her eyes. They gazed at each other. "She picked up all the clues and put them together."

"There were dreams, Mom... and—"

"I'm sure there *were*, angel," said her mother, stroking her cheeks, her forehead. "Ever since you were tiny you've been a busy sleeper. Our dreams knit together so many disparate strands and solve our problems for us! Things we pick up unconsciously in everyday life—our dreams make sense of it all."

"But it was more than that, Mom—"

"Let's not forget our boy Finn, here," cut in Billy, presenting him as if for a ribbon or trophy. "He found the first of the pieces of eight."

"Well, Finn is simply indispensable," Kate responded, placing a hand on his silky blond head. "We couldn't manage without him."

Christmas holidays had started early for Sappho and Finn. They hadn't been back to Gray Star Elementary since finding the coins. The A-frame was crowded and noisy—with preparations for Christmas, with Alice's cycle of cries, with the racket of Cowboy Cal's reno work on the chicken coop, with Billy's stoking of the stove, with Kate's cooking. Just now they were seated around the dining table making decorations. Sappho was scissoring paper angels and flying horses in white, then detailing their many wing-feathers with silver and gold paint. Next she would make stars, and snowflakes—starflakes, even.

She had brought out her special collection of green and blue glass beads and beach treasure to make presents. Finn and Billy were threading popcorn and cranberries into long strings to hang around the cabin and on the fragrant spruce tree they had cut in the forest. Kate had Alice snuffling at her breast. Outside the rain was pouring down and it was getting dark at three in the afternoon, but inside it was bright and warm.

The stove was crackling hard and they had lit candles as well as the kerosene lamps.

"When's the big meeting, Billy?" asked Kate.

"Day after tomorrow." He would be going to the longhouse to speak with Chief Raphael and two archaeologists from the University of British Columbia. Dan Joe would be there too.

"Is that going to complicate things, having Dan there?"

"Nope. If I'm right, Dan Joe will be there to make sure this silver leaves Gray Star forever."

"Will you bring all twelve coins to the longhouse?"

"Put it this way, Katie. I hafta keep my cards close to my chest at this point."

She cleared her throat. "Well, Canada does have a say in what becomes of those coins, you know."

"Hmm... Billy Black: Pirate or Privateer? How will historians remember me?" He rubbed his beard and stared at the rafters in lieu of the sky.

"Billy! It's not a joke."

"It's not? Aw, relax, Katie. Keep your hair on. Canada will have her say. Canada has a strong representative right here in this cabin..."

The following afternoon Billy returned to the A-frame and stuffed everyone's pockets full of candy-canes and colourful foil-wrapped chocolate Santas. Kate, who got the biggest chocolate Santa, made only the smallest of protests.

"What happened at the meeting, Billy?" she asked, unwinding the foil from her Santa's hat and nibbling away.

"I called my supervisor at Berkeley from the pay-phone at the General Store. He thought his ears were playing tricks on him—that's how long I've been out of touch."

"Was that before the meeting or after?"

"After."

"Well? And? What happened there?"

"We worked it all out. I agreed to hand over half the silver to U.B.C. in exchange for their guarantee that they won't display it until I've submitted my thesis. We did hammer out a deadline for that, though. Two years. Ah—a deadline'll do me good."

"And what about the band? The natives?"

"The Chief and Dan butted heads over the question of compensation. They agree that the coins need to get outta Gray Star, but when the Chief heard that both universities would pony up cash, he got interested—talked about building something with it. But Dan thinks that amounts to the same thing. Still blood money, as far as he's concerned. Says the curse won't lift until the pirate silver has been returned, period. The Chief's the chief, and he's talkin' bingo hall, community centre, but Dan Joe... is a force to be reckoned with. Doesn't want that money for *any* purpose, nohow. I bet he'll get his way."

"Wow. So what's next?"

He wrapped his arms around Kate, who already had her arms wrapped around Alice. "It's December 20th. What's next is that in four days we have a big Christmas dinner, open our gifts, and then open our suitcases and pack them. We're hittin' the road. First stop, Vancouver. And then if we drive seriously, we can make it to Frisco in twenty-four hours."

Billy went to the door and opened it. "I gotta find us a VW camper van. All the hard-up hippies around these parts, shouldn't be too hard."

The day they left Gray Star, Cowboy Cal was officially in charge of Chickenland. Wearing his new black Stetson, a gift they had all—the family, the Mounties, the Volunteer Fire Department, the Taylors, even Blow-Yer-Brains-Out Bob—chipped in for, Cal saw them off from the front porch of the cabin. He looked cosy in a heavy Cowichan sweater, patterned in cream, gray and beige, which Maureen had given him. "Remember, Cal, the A-frame is *your* house," Billy yelled out the driver's window of their latest VW van. "Don't let those birds get ideas above their station. Look what happened to me when I let my guard down,"

"Don't you worry. I'm holdin' the fort," Cal called back, his voice brimming with confidence.

They all waved to Cal as Billy pulled the van out of the clearing. "You think *I* was chicken-whipped? Mark my words," Billy whispered, "they'll have him relegated to a tent in the yard within a week. They'll drive him out of the cabin AND the coop."

The day they left Gray Star they detoured to the Stables so that Sappho could give Barb, who was grooming black Zorro to a high shine, a hug good-bye. "I'm wearing the t-shirt you gave me for Christmas, Barb," said Sappho, opening her jean-jacket to reveal the pristine cap-sleeved top the Taylors had brought her from Town—Grouse Mountain Sky-Ride, it read. "Don't be

sad, sweetheart! Me 'n Russ *love* California! We'll pick you kids up in San Francisco and drive you down the coast to Disneyland."

The day they left Gray Star they stopped by to see a lot of people—Bob, Maureen, Ruth, Mr. Mahoney, the Mounties and the various members of the Volunteer Fire Department. The strange thing was, though, that later on Sappho kept thinking she could see them all in the ferry line-up. Though they had set out in plenty of time to meet the 10:05 a.m., the highway seemed much more crowded than usual, and a lot of cars and trucks were tugging trailers and had their roof-racks piled high. Sappho thought she saw several horse-trailers. The fog was settling in, so it was hard to be sure.

As they drove over the bridge and slowly through the Rez, they were surprised to find the Coast Highway was lined on both sides with Indians—thinly at first, but more thickly as people trickled out of the houses to stand at the roadside, responding to some inaudible message. Elders emerged from the little houses, some supported by the young and strong. Various kids turned up, some on bicycles and tricycles. Apparently every inhabitant of the reservation had turned out to watch them and the rest of the ferry traffic pass. It was like being in a parade, though none of the onlookers were smiling and waving. Neither were they scowling. Their faces were illegible. Sappho saw Chief Raphael. A few yards further she saw Dan Joe. She saw Michael, his hands shoved into the pockets of his ski-jacket. She followed him with her eyes and looked back, but he did not turn his head.

It seemed to take a long time to get through the Rez, though the people were not blocking traffic. Time just stretched out as they drove by, bearing most of their belongings and twelve pieces of Spanish silver. And when Sappho turned around again, hoping in vain for a last glimpse of Michael Joe, she perceived that the ferry traffic trailed far, far behind them. She could not see an end to it.

"It's winter," said Kate. "I've never seen so many people trying to get to the Mainland in winter. Could it be the Christmas holidays?"

"Maybe," replied Billy. Ferry workers in their orange neon vests were working their way down through the lanes of traffic on foot. They held radios, and some of them had bullhorns. Billy rolled down his window and waved one young man over. "What's goin' on?"

"They're putting on more sailings. That's all I can say at this time," he told them. "You'll probably make it on to the 11:10."

"But we left early!" said Kate.

"Yes, ma'am. However, it appears that many other folks had the very same idea." His radio crackled, and he listened to it. "And from what it sounds like, you are among the lucky ones. Some of these people won't get out until supper-time—that's how long the line-up is now. The last ferry to the Mainland is 9 p.m., and I plan to be on that one myself. We leave 'er in Horseshoe Bay for the night." He trundled on his way, spreading the news.

The fog was damp, and soon rain was blurring the windshield. "Lucky these things work," said Billy, prodding the wipers to life. Now the rain was sticking and bunching up on the wipers.

"Snow!" cried Finn, who had never seen snow.

"It hardly ever snows in Gray Star," said Kate in a soft monotone, and Sappho and Billy nodded in unison.

Finn was right, though. Thickening flakes were whirling down in the form of tiny twisters. Through the whitening air Sappho saw the ferry approach the dock, its long rows of windows lit up, though it was not yet noon. The huge boat sounded its warning blast—a warning to smaller craft, to floating birds, to inattentive passengers and employees alike. "The Queen of Nanaimo," she read aloud. It docked and, in the rising wind, docking was quite an ordeal. The boat went a little wide of the wharf and pitched from rubber buffer to rubber buffer for a while before coming at length to the properly centred position. There was a lot of shrieking and creaking of metal. Finally, the ferry was flush with the ramp, and the crew began to chain it to the dock and then to draw back the gates. Now they would see the long line of cars, trucks, camper-vans and Greyhound buses emerge, emptying the ferry so they could drive on.

Save one decrepit Chevrolet containing several Joe cousins, the hold was empty.

The ferry workers flew into action, giving elaborate hand-signals to the lone Chevy. After checking with their radios that this was indeed the sum total of northbound traffic, they began beckoning the long lines of south-bound vehicles into the ship. With the snow whirling and rapidly thickening around them, the stunned drivers bore slowly and hesitantly down on their gas-pedals, braking gently every few feet to avoid skidding,

After a while it was Billy's turn to drive carefully down the ramp and into the body of the ship. It was warm in the van and cold without.They stayed below deck and ate the picnic lunch Kate had fixed—turkey sandwiches and other Christmas leftovers. Alice slept. No-one said any-thing about the strange parade through the Rez. Or the endless ferry lineup behind them, or the familiar faces they had seemed to spot in that lineup. No-one men-tioned the virtually empty arriving ship, or how crowded this one was.

When they arrived at Horseshoe Bay, they realized they had slept through the rest of the voyage.

"Turkey makes people drowsy," said Kate. "My mother always said that."

Horseshoe Bay was alive with sharp winter sunshine. There was no trace of snow. Now, as they drove off the ferry and up towards the Upper Levels Highway leading to Vancouver and beyond, Sappho turned to catch a last view of the Gray Star stretch of coast, where life had been such a strong mixture of sweet and salt. But of that coast nothing was visible: a dense fog or snow-cloud had grown denser, had unfurled like a massive curtain to conceal Gray Star altogether. A person could be forgiven, she told herself, for thinking that the place had disappeared.

Up, up went the van and onto the Upper Levels Highway. She turned around in time to see the arm of Point Grey stretching out. "That's U.B.C.," said Billy, pointing. We'll have to make a stop there. Grouse Mountain's up over there," he went on, in honour of Sappho's prized new t-shirt. Soon they could see the colourfully painted wooden ranks of Kitsilano houses and the tall glass buildings of downtown. They approached they delicate orange spans of Lions Gate Bridge with its arrangement of many vertiginous ladders. Lions Gate took them through Stanley Park ("Look back quick!" said Kate, and Sappho and Finn saw the huge stone lions that guarded the bridge), past Lost Lagoon, and into the mild urban charms of Vancouver. Soon would come other places—Washington State, the Oregon coast, California. "When night falls in Vancouver, you'll see the most wonderful Christmas lights—every colour in the spectrum, every crazy design imaginable," promised Kate. "And that *almost* compensates for the way that the urban light pollution snuffs out the stars by night."

Sappho took her mother's hand and smiled, thinking to herself that for now, at least, that was a trade-off she was happy to make.

Justine Brown was born in Vancouver and has travelled widely. She studied literature and earned an M.A. from the University of Toronto. She is the author of Hollywood Utopia and All Possible Worlds (New Star Books). She lives in London, England with her husband.